The Untrodden Path

The Untrodden Path
Edited & Compiled by
Vaishali Chandorkar Chitale

Paperback Edition

First published in India in 2023 by

Inkfeathers Publishing
Vivek Vihar, New Delhi 110095
www.inkfeathers.com

ISBN 978-81-19483-02-0

The Untrodden Path

Edited & Compiled by

Vaishali Chandorkar Chitale

Inkfeathers Publishing
www.inkfeathers.com

Disclaimer

The anthology "The Untrodden Path" is a collection of 22 short stories and 11 poems written by 27 authors who belong to different parts of the world.

Unless otherwise indicated, all the names, characters, objects, businesses, places, events, incidents—whether physical/non-physical, real/unreal, tangible/ intangible in whatsoever description used in this book are either the product of the author's imagination or used in a fictitious manner. Any resemblance to actual persons, objects, entities, living or dead, or actual events is purely coincidental.

The contents published in this book are solely owned by their respective authors and are in no way intended to hurt anyone's religious, political, spiritual, brand, personal or fanatic beliefs and/or faith, whatsoever. In case, any sort of plagiarism is detected in the contents within this anthology or in case of any complaints, grievances, or objections, neither the anthology editor nor the publisher is to be held responsible.

Curated with the writings of

Kirti V, Rupali Samant, Augusta Vimla Vincent,

Asad Chaugule, Binta Elsa Biju, Praneel Dev,

Anthony Fernandes, Rhythmi Rosa S, Ishita Sharma,

Mehak Lakhwani, Col Gaurav Bhatia PhD (Retd),

Col Arun Hariharan, Beji Mathews, Vivek Gulati,

Dr. Raj Shankar Ghosh, Shirley Verghese, Rita Som,

Dr. Neelam Singh, Dr. Neeta Sanghvi Ranbhan,

Vasudha Kapoor Duggal, Aditi Lahiry, Monika Patel,

Ramya V, Zeyd Ladha, Vaishali Chandorkar Chitale

Contents

About the Editor

Vaishali Chandorkar Chitale

'Life is never single dimensional as we all know,
We have to experience happiness, loss and heartache
for us to live and grow.'

These lines, written by Vaishali in her poem, "Beautiful Life" defines her oeuvre. She believes in living each moment and savouring every aspect that life has to offer. She realised early on that life is not just a bed of roses, but it has its shares of thorns too. Her writing—short stories and poems—reflects this very reality.

A graduate of English literature from Hindu College, Delhi University and an alumna of IIMC (Journalism) she has covered human interest stories for various publications which helped her develop her writing and observation skills. She has worked as an educator and moulded young minds to fight injustice and to live with honour. A prolific writer, her stories and poems have won many awards and certificates and have been published in many paperbacks to date.

Her debut book of poems, "Whispers of Immortality" published in 2022, has garnered rave reviews by poetry lovers and adorn many a book shelves.

A freelance editor, she has seven anthologies to her credit and more in the pipeline.

From the Editor's desk

The genesis of this book is the poem, 'The Road Not Taken' written by Robert Frost. This poem has stayed with me ever since I studied it in school, and it has shaped most of my life choices. I have often wondered about them in retrospect, for some came straight from the heart and some with deliberate thought. Though I have lived not to regret the walk that I walked; inevitably sometimes, 'What if?' creeps in unbidden. This dilemma of 'what could have been', led me to conceptualise this anthology.

From soul-stirring poems to poignant stories that prod you to take a closer look at life, this book has it all. Immerse yourselves in the exceptional journeys that these writers dared to take and live a life most extraordinary. Their inspiring stories motivating us to think 'out-of-the-box' is what characterises this book.

This anthology is a heart-warming read, and I am sure you will treasure it for a long time to come.

Happy Reading.

Vaishali Chandorkar Chitale

Editor

Untrodden Path—An Acrostic

@Kirti V

Unusual for many,
New for some,
Treacherous or interesting,
Ravines or roads,
Outlaws one might become,
Deciding the path and
Decoding the route,
Engulfed, we might be, or
Nestled in its warmth.

Paths of life,
Amaze us through out,
Testing us time and again and
Heralding our attempt at it.

I Don't Want to be a Goddess

Col Arun Hariharan

Kanta's whole family was in the fields, busy picking cotton from the ripe crop standing there. They were farmers who lived in a small village called Chandori near Nasik, which lay along the banks of the great river Godavari. It was a critical time since the traders from Nasik and Poona would be arriving in just a few weeks to purchase the cotton and pay for it in gold and silver coins. All hands of the family—be they young or old—were toiling in the field as work was at its peak.

But Kanta was not there. Instead, she was sitting by the banks of the Godavari, staring at the river's mighty waters and absentmindedly flinging stones into it. She yawned in a bored manner. She was sick and tired of this mundane routine year after year which she had been following for the nine years that she had spent with her husband Bhimrao's family ...she was almost twenty-one now.

Her father, Shantarao, was a hardworking man who had a modest holding of eighty *bighas*[1] of fertile land in the Village of Dadegaon, South of the Godavari. Her family being reasonably well-to-do, Kanta had enjoyed a decent childhood along with her other four

[1] 1 bigha is approximately equal to ½ Acre.

siblings, three elder sisters, and one little brother. She was an aberration of sorts, being the only girl child in her family to have received some form of education. Her grandfather, Baburao, was an ardent devotee of Saint Eknath[1] of the *Varakari Sampradaya*[2] and had been a regular participant for many years in the *Vaaris*[3] organized by the Sampradaya. She happened to be one of the only three girl pupils at the Gurukul run by the venerable Pandit Someshwar, a Varakari himself, the progressive man who had prevailed upon her grandfather to send little Kanta to school. For seven years, she went to the gurukul every day—on strict instructions to her parents by Baburao—whilst her sisters toiled in domestic work.

The years of education under Panditji, learning about noble saints, great kings, and the vile Mughal invaders from the North, had made her aware and worldly-wise. However, her parents were severely worried. "Who will marry her now?" Shalinitai, her weary mother, would worriedly ask her father. "She is disinterested in housework and does not like working in the fields. What use is all this learning for a girl?"

As were the norms, she was betrothed to Bhimrao, also of an agrarian family from Chandori, a village North of the Godavari, when she was all of eight and thereafter married him when she was ten. Life dealt a double blow on her when she was twelve when old Baburao died of Cholera while on one of his Vaaris, and her parents decided to send her to Chandori to be with her husband. "Your

---

[1] Sant Eknath (c. 1533 – c. 1599), was a Marathi Hindu saint, philosopher, and poet. He was a devotee of the Hindu deity Krishna and is a major figure of the Warkari tradition. Eknath is often viewed as a spiritual successor to the prominent Marathi saints Dnyaneshwar and Namdev.

[2] Varkari is a sect within the bhakti spiritual tradition of Hinduism, geographically associated with the Indian state of Maharashtra. Varkaris worship Vitthal, the presiding deity of Pandharpur, regarded as a form of Krishna.

[3] Religious gathering

sisters are all in their husbands' places from the time they were married. How long do you want to be with us? Bhimrao's family is not taking it kindly to you staying on here and going to Gurukul. Moreover, the neighbours have also started passing remarks on you attending school with boys, having been married for two years and more," said her father brushing aside her protests regarding her wanting to continue school.

With a heavy heart, Kanta left her beloved Dadegaon and bid a tearful farewell to her family and her little kid brother.

Her initial days in Bhimrao's household had not been bad. Her in-laws were simple, God-fearing, and respected people who tried their best to make her feel comfortable. Moreover, she was a pretty-looking, fair, and tall girl—a very sought—after combination for an ideal daughter-in-law. She, however, still missed Panditji and the wonderful moments she spent at the Gurukul. Three years later, her marital union with Bhimrao was physically consummated, and by the time she was all of fifteen years and ten months, she had a little girl child—Savitri in her lap.

Kanta now busied herself with taking care of the child, the family and helping in the fields, if required. She, however, continued to keep up her reading—gobbling up whatever came her way—be it religious discourses of Eknath, books on basic arithmetic, Marathi grammar, and so on. This little effort in self-education continued through years in which she not only weathered a miscarriage and the birth of another child (Waman—a boy this time) by the time she was eighteen.

"Kanta! Where are you?" she heard the youthful voice of Bhimrao call out for her. She knew her little private time was now over and sighed as she moved in the direction from which she heard her husband's voice. Bhimrao, covered with sweat and cotton fluff, lithe and sun burnt, did sound a little angry when he asked her: "You have again drifted off! Waman is crying from hunger, and there is so much work left. I don't know what has come over you." Kanta did not say anything and timidly followed him back to the fields.

It was way past dusk when the family reached back home and had a hearty dinner. Everyone retired to bed early as they had an early and long day coming up.

Kanta's sleep was broken in the wee hours of the next morning by sounds of wailing and lamenting. She got up with a start and peered out of the window. She saw a motley crowd gathered outside their neighbour Kushalbhau's house. She saw that Bhimrao was still asleep beside her. Not wanting to disturb him, she tip-toed out of the house to find out the cause of the agitation. As she went closer, to her horror, she found Sampatrao, Kushalbhau's son, who must have been around twenty years lying on the ground, covered in a white sheet, apparently dead. It emerged that he had been unwell for the last two days with a high fever and had passed away in the night. Shaku, Sampatrao's young wife (who probably was a couple of years younger than Kanta), already distraught with grief, was undergoing the painful ritual of bangle breaking and tonsuring of her head, as though the pain of losing her young husband was not enough for her.

Kanta came back home with a disturbed mind. After a while, she was startled out of her stupor by the shrill cries of Shaku. She ran out of the house and saw a hideous scene of the pitiable-looking Shaku dressed up as a bride being forced into a bullock cart and the young widow resisting and screaming, whereas a number of villagers, including Bhimrao and his father prostrating before her and chanting "*Sati Mata ki Jai*!". "What happened, mother?" She inquired from her mother-in-law. "Nothing, Shaku is a blessed one. I wonder why she is resisting in performing her divine duty. She has been blessed to become a Sati Mata and get consigned on the pyre of Sampatrao." Kanta was horrified. She had heard about the practice of Sati but had never seen it being practiced up close. "But this is cruel and wrong. Why should she be burnt on the pyre? She has done no wrong, and she does not want to become a Sati in any case," she blurted out. Her mother-in-law was horrified. "Shut up! Who are you to comment on this. Come inside lest someone hears you. How dare you speak such blasphemous words? You are but a woman and have no right to speak like this." Kanta could not take it anymore, and continued— "Mother, nowhere does our religion say that a widow must burn at the pyre of her husband against her will. Do you know our Nasik region was one of the most progressive societies for women during the Vedic ages? Women were even involved in running the government. Come, let's go and stop them before they murder Shaku..." Her talk was cut by a tight slap on the back of her head. She turned around to see her father-in-law standing there, livid with anger. "Do we now have to hear discourses from the women of our house about our traditions? Kanta is not at fault, but her parents—and that damned Panditji who has filled her mind with garbage. Bhim, tell your wife if she utters one more word, I will cut off her tongue." He gave her another painful slap on her cheeks as a parting shot and stomped off.

Only Bhimrao's father and uncles went to Sampatrao's funeral— where Shaku, in all her bridal finery, was elevated to a Goddess— all a cruel twist of fate combined with heartless superstition.

Two days passed with Kanta in a melancholy mood. It rained a little the following day. Luckily it cleared out soon, and the family left for the fields. A large number of extra labourers had been hired to hasten the harvest and tie the bales. Bhimrao was busy animatedly shouting out instructions to the hired hands. Kanta, still dazed by the experience of a few days back, was trying to get back to the grid. Soon everyone was deeply engrossed in work, fully knowing that the buyers from Nasik would be arriving very shortly. Suddenly, Kanta heard a loud yell from the direction in which the men were working and, along with her mother-in-law, rushed toward the source of the sound. To her horror, she found Bhimrao clutching his right forearm and writhing on the ground screaming plaintively. There was a commotion all around, and she could not comprehend the reason for the agitation. Suddenly, Bhimrao began frothing from his mouth and started having convulsions. "He has been bitten by a Krait!" screamed the foreman, quick somebody gets the *Vaid* (village doctor). The snake had sneaked into the harvested cotton, probably because of the morning rain, and had bitten Bhimrao on his forearm as he was helping some labourers sift the cotton. In a matter of minutes, the convulsions abruptly stopped even as the horrified onlookers helplessly looked on and the foreman was trying to cut and clear the bite area. In just three days since she saw Shaku widowed-—the unthinkable had happened—Kanta, not yet all of twenty-one, was herself a widow now.

The time after that passed like a bad dream, with her remembering only bits and pieces—women lamenting, men folk cursing, and her two little children not comprehending what the fuss was all about. In her trance-like state, she was made to relive all the gory rituals of bangle breaking and tonsuring she had seen Shaku undergo just sometime back. Finally, the arrangements for the funeral of Bhimrao were made, and a pyre was erected on the banks of the Godavari. The time had come for Kanta to attain divine status; she was bathed by the women folk of the household and dressed in bridal finery. Drained emotionally and physically, she passed out before the funeral and had to be carried in a palanquin to the location of the pyre. The pyre was ready, and the air was thick with the shouts of "*Ram Naam Satya Hain*"[1] and "*Sati Mata ki jai*." The priest motioned that everything was ready, and the body of Bhimrao was placed on the pyre. Someone then sprinkled cold water on the face of Kanta to revive her from her swoon; she groggily got up and looked around. Suddenly, she seemed very aware of her surroundings and the fate that awaited her. "No, I don't want to die!" she screamed. "You stupid woman, you should not say such

[1] God's name is the final truth.

things…you are going to be a Goddess very soon; come on, hurry up and sit on the pyre!" thundered the portly priest. In a split second, Kanta thought, "I don't want to be burnt to death on the pyre; I rather consign myself to Mother Godavari…," and before any of the people around realised anything, she ran and jumped into the swirling waters of Godavari. As the current dragged her away and she could hear people shouting and screaming on the banks and someone jumping into the water. A floating log of wood bumped her head, and she passed out.

When she opened her eyes, she found her surroundings dark. At first, she could not remember what had happened, and then the memories of her past came back to her in a flash. She got up to a sitting position and looked around; she was in some kind of tent or hut. Suddenly, someone from the other end of the hut got up and lit an oil lantern, and asked in a kindly voice: "How are you feeling, child?" She saw the benevolent face of an old woman in the flickering light. Uhhh...my head hurts! Where am I?" "Don't worry; you are safe. We found you lying senseless on the banks of Godavari. I will just go inform the *Rani* (queen)…she was very concerned about you." The old lady left the hut and came back after some time with some fruits and a warm glass of milk. "Eat this child; it will help you recover faster!". Just then, another woman came in and announced that Rani was coming to see her. A few minutes later, an elegant old lady with two torch bearers entered the hut and touched Kanta's head very kindly. "Such a beautiful girl! I wonder what tragedy befell her. Rest now, my child; you can come and meet me tomorrow when you feel better."

After a fitful sleep, the morning dawned, and the old lady gave her a fresh pair of clothes and helped her dress up. She told her that the "Rani" who had visited her last night was none other than Rajmata[1] Jijabai, the mother of the Great Maratha Warrior Shivaji,

[1] Queen Mother

who had routed Bijapur Sultan's vast armies. The Rajmata, despite her advanced years, had a regal presence. "You are lucky, my child! She said, "My entourage was going from Nasik to Nanded, and one of my Sipahis[1] found you lying on the riverside, barely breathing. You have Mata Godavari's blessings! Tell me what happened. Do not fear for anything." Kanta blurted out all that had happened to her and to Shaku, herself surprised at her own courage and energy, considering that these were probably the first words she spoke after her 're-birth'. Jijabai heard her in rapt attention without any interruption. By the time Kanta finished, she felt totally drained and was sobbing. The Rani got up and kindly patted her cheeks and said, "Don't cry, my child! What you did was just great.... Even I could not gather the courage to take a stand as you did when my husband, Raja Shahaji, died two years back. But for my noble son Shiva who dissuaded me from committing Sati, I too would have been consigned to the pyre of my husband. I am now convinced that this practice is barbaric and degrades the very spirit of womanhood."

Surprising herself, Kanta replied to the Rani, "Rani Sahiba, our land, great Maharashtra, was known for empowering its women even in the Vedic period and during the reign of the Satvahanas when Nasik flourished as a great centre of learning and knowledge." The Rani was amazed. "You speak beyond your age, girl! You seem quite learned." Kanta told her about her days with Panditji back in her village and her self-education. The Rani was truly impressed. "We definitely need more young people like you to build a brighter future for our kingdom. Appoint her as my personal chambermaid from here on," said the Rani, motioning to one of the important-looking courtiers standing there.

Kanta lived with the Rani until the latter's death in 1674, after which the newly crowned Chhatrapati Shivaji made her in charge of a girls-only Gurukul in Nasik—a first of its kind, where she spread

[1] Soldiers

the treasure of knowledge and empowerment to little girls. Also, one of the first steps taken by Shivaji after his coronation was the abolition of Sati in his *Rajya* (Kingdom), a decision probably somewhere influenced by the real-life tale of a helpless young girl who refused to be burnt at her husband's pyre many years ago.

Kanta was contented but knew that she could never ever visit her beloved Dadegaon or Chandori and meet her family or children as her 'disgrace' in the village on that fateful day would have made sure that her name would have been erased forever from the memories of her kith and kin and in any case, her unfortunate children were too young to even remember how she looked like. But every time she looked at the swirling waters of the Godavari, she knew the mighty river understood her sorrow only as a mother could.

*****

Disclaimer: Though this story features certain historical characters and timelines, it is purely fictional and a work of the Author's imagination.

A River

Dr. Raj Shankar Ghosh

On a late March afternoon, a river stopped flowing.

Leaves rustled. Sparrows flew. The sun eventually set. Weary folks walked back home. A day's work done. Night fell. The boys went to bed. Girls had dreams.

A river, in the meantime, had stopped flowing.

My father was in Government service. He had recently been transferred to a small town. "A smaller living quarter in my new posting," he announced over dinner one November day. "We may not have space for all. The furniture."

The furniture was dumped in a lonely room on the roof of our ancestral house. Some seven hundred miles away. Kolkata. I was admitted to a boarding school. On a late March afternoon. Some seven hundred miles away. Kolkata again.

Everything changed. The prayer. The food. The mattress. English. Bland. Hard. In that order.

Days moved on. Nights rolled on.

One April morning, the dates for the School Exhibition were announced. Dates in May. "You must participate. There will be prizes. For the best demonstrator for each subject. This is an opportunity for you to know your friends and your friends to know you." Principal Sir spoke in the school assembly that day.

Lunch break. I was walking back alone. I met Principal Sir in front of the mango orchard. He smiled. He beckoned. "Are you, not the new boy who has joined this summer?" he asked. I wanted to correct him. But he continued, "Which department have you chosen to participate in?" I wanted to tell him the truth. But 'Geography', I said. He patted me on the back. "Know your country, and you shall know the world." He blessed. His palm was up on my scalp by then. I wanted to tell him, 'Pardon?' then. I want to tell him, 'Pardon? Now. But he walked away. I stood wondering. My country. The world. So different. Yet, if I know one, I know the other. He had said.

I registered for a project in the geography department late afternoon of the same day. As I returned to my hostel, the sun was setting. I walked on dry leaves by the orchard. School staff were on their way back home. I was walking in the opposite direction.

I was assigned my project the next morning. "You will work on the river Ganga, from her origin to her confluence. Choose your board, your clay, and your plastic," the teacher said. "Who will be my friends for the project?" I asked. Perplexed. The whole purpose was to know my friends and my friends to know me. "This is not like going back from school alone with leaves beneath my feet and a sweet smell lingering in the air," I thought. "Oh, this shall be a standalone project. You will stand alone to demonstrate," the teacher said. A few laughed. A few smiled. A few stared. The rest did not really care. I took my bag. Cardboard. A white poster paper. Pastel. Plastic trees, houses, and temples.

Crayon. Pins. Tiny red, blue, and yellow flags. Pencil. Glue. Scale. Eraser.

For the next four days, the river flowed in full steam. Splashing against the rocks. Overflowing the concrete steps at the banks. Listening to the little ripples, little boys made swimming.

Overhearing the stories that their mothers told. And when all fell silent, when it was dark all around, the river listened to its own songs. For the rest whom the river heard were strangers.

The project took seven days to complete.

On the eighth day, there was an inspection by the head of our geography department. I coloured the mountain green. The river is blue. The plastic temples were houses and temples. Red flag for the temples. Yellow flags for the houses. Blue flags for the rest. I had two blue flags with me. The inspector came at seven pm. Or somewhere around that time, when the lights were on, and the sun had set. He came. He saw. And he kicked. One kick on the cardboard. And the flags went down the stairs. The houses collapsed. The mountain fell. It was all a mass of dirty crumbles scattered on the stairs. "This is nonsense," the head said. And he walked away.

A river stopped flowing that day on an evening in May.

I sat there at the top of the stairs. Vacant. Blank. Not knowing what to do. This was my chance to know my friends. My friends to know me. It was shattered. It was nonsense, as the Headteacher had said. "How will I know my friends?" I sat at the top of the stairs and asked myself.

I do not know for how long the river stood still. It could have been seconds, minutes, or hours. The night was darker. The lights in the hall were brighter. The silence around louder.

A hand came upon the river's chest. A warm fleshy palm. And a voice asked, "Why cry, my child?" Slowly I raised my head. In pristine white attire, someone stood before me. Hazy. Then I recognized. Head, English Department. I stood up. To acknowledge his presence. I told him the story of the earthquake. A man-made disaster. The temple. The mountain. The river. The houses. Scattered. "It was nonsense," I said. He smiled. He lifted me up by my shoulders. He made me stand erect. He lifted my chin. And in a solemn voice, said. "Your path to success has begun. You have tasted failure."

He took me with him to the English Department. I registered as a demonstrator in that department. “GBS. George Bernard Shaw shall be your project. Pygmalion. And you will work with him.” A boy taller than me stood where he pointed. I liked him. He wore square glasses. He smiled and waved. I had found a friend. I smiled. I waved too.

The river flowed again for the next seven days. The river flowed in the library. The river flowed in the assembly. The river found its way into the English department. The day of the exhibition came sometime in May.

Our stall was a favour. The visitors favoured us by visiting our stall, entertaining us with witty remarks from Shaw, and encouraging us to pursue English literature. Then came the band of judges. They laughed. They smiled. They patted. “Good boys. You have mastered your English well.” And they went. Three days later, the exhibition ended. My friend and I had won the best demonstrator award from the English Department. They gave prizes. We were invited to the stage.

A river stopped flowing momentarily. And then, who knows from where the water came? The river splashed forward. Overflowing the banks. Turning the boats that sailed. And beckoning big men and women who stood at the bank for a swim. The river knew them. They knew the river now.

The river never stopped flowing again.

Roop

Neelam Singh

The night of Diwali slowly slipped into the wee hours of the morning. Shukra was lying quietly on the mud-tiled roofed terrace of his small house, gazing wildly at the dim stars of the dark Amavasya (no moon) night.

It had been a busy festive day. *Laxmi Pooja* (prayers to Hindu Goddess Laxmi) had been performed by the women folk of the house. Children were busy with the crackers, and now, as the lights and *diyas* faded away and he was still wide awake. His mind drifted away into the events of the last Diwali and even further down memory lane to the time when he was a young boy.

He was thirteen years old and studying in standard VII of the local school in the Khatlene village of the Jaisalmer district of Rajasthan. His parents had selected a bride for him—Roop, eight years old, from a nearby village. He had been excited about the event when his baraat proceeded to his would-be bride's village.

The ceremonies over, he had received colourful clothes and gifts and had the first glimpse of Roop in her bright, brilliant outfit. Then the baraat had returned home, and he was back to his routine of farming and schooling. Roop had stayed behind.

Seven years later, there were celebrations again, and he had finally brought his wife home, and the days that followed were full of joy and excitement.

Soon Roop gave birth to their first daughter. Shukra was not happy; he had expected a son. He felt that Roop had let him down in front of his *baradari* (community).

In the years that followed, Roop gave birth to their second, third, and fourth daughters, and along with each female child, his happiness and love for his wife faded into oblivion. In his frustration, he kept cursing and beating her. Now at the age of twenty-four, being pregnant for the fifth time, she was terrified and scared mentally and physically. She became very weak and shattered. If she gave birth to a female child again, she would never be pardoned. A dim ray of hope of giving him a 'son' kept her going for nine months.

At last, the D-day arrived. It was the day of Diwali when she started getting labour pains. She was put into the dark corner of the house, and then as the pain became unbearable, a *local dai* (midwife) was called who conducted the delivery; to the utter disappointment of everyone in the house, a little Laxmi was born on the day of *Laxmi Pooja.*

Roop could not hold back her tears. No one in the house visited her the whole day, and she kept thinking about the unpardonable sins she must have committed for begetting daughter after daughter. The day after dawned, Shukra's mother entered her room and surprisingly found a deathly silence. There was no sign of her daughter-in-law or the newborn baby. Suddenly the whole house was awake, and Roop's dead body, along with her newborn baby, was found in the well of the *angan* (courtyard) of the house.

The police were informed, and the legal procedure was followed. The final verdict was given that Roop had strangulated her own child and then jumped to her death in the well.

In a month's time, Shukra married a sixteen-year Rivoli, and soon he was blessed with the birth of a son. This time there was a lot of rejoicing in the house, and the four little girls, too, enjoyed the whole celebration, forgetting their mother by now.

As Shukra lay with his wife and the newborn son, his mind was in utter turmoil. Had Roop really committed suicide? Had he driven her to it by his boorish and nasty behaviour? His anger against her for giving him daughter after daughter? Had she walked this untrodden path just because she blamed herself for not begetting a son? Was it, not his responsibility to help Roop to flower into womanhood and motherhood? Was it, not his responsibility to keep her happy? Had he not failed her? But did she ever make him feel like a failure? No, she, to her last day on this Earth, served him to the best of her abilities.

Was it only her responsibility or fault for producing daughters, and why was the birth of a girl shunned? Guilt gnawed at him. He knew the sex of the baby was decided by the male sperm, and a woman had no hand in its gender formation. Why did he make her feel that she had failed him by not giving him a son? They had four beautiful daughters: why this insistence on having a son? Haven't daughters proved today that they are equal to any son? That they are equally capable of not only looking after themselves but their families and parents too?

Roop. His wife. His wife, whom he had married young and made her go through five pregnancies without a break. His wife, whom he was morally and ethically responsible for. His wife, whom he had fallen in love with on seeing her for the first time. His wife, whom he had pledged to protect from all harm. His wife, the mother of his four daughters!

Had she committed the murder of her baby, was this the road God had paved for her to trod on, or had she walked into the path that should have remained untrodden? These questions swirled in his mind and made him restless.

Though it was her hands that strangulated the baby, was Shukra not equally responsible for the death of his baby and the wife? Why were the societal pressures so high as to lead a woman to such a miserable end? Why should a woman sacrifice her life for no fault of hers? Why did he make it impossible for her to live? Who was responsible for these two deaths? Was it Roop who killed her daughter, or was it Shukra who killed both?

But then, should Shukra live as if he had not committed a crime? He, too, had failed her, but she was the only one who paid for failing; if you call her delivering healthy daughters, an act of failure!

These thoughts kept Shukra awake night after night.

*****

Meanwhile, his new wife and his son were sleeping peacefully by his side, blissfully unaware that they, too, had narrowly escaped a fate like Roop's.

Love. Dream. Aim. Success. History.

@Rhythmi Rosa S

Loving passionate dreams
It is better than falling for mere deviations.
Dreams push brains and hearts.
To achieve glittery success sparks.
They create indestructible stories.
In the world of undying history.
So choose your destiny with wisdom
Without throwing your aims at the infinite random.

The Silver Lining

Beji Mathews

The final heave was successful. There was thunderous applause from the onlookers, and Johny had tears of joy in his eyes. After the referee confirmed the lift, Johny dropped the weights and left the stage with a cheerful welcome from a few teammates and his team manager.

The event was the World Power Lifting Championship being held in South Africa. Since Power Lifting is not part of the Olympic Games and because other major World events were also being held in close vicinity, the hall was not completely full; however, there was a sizeable audience.

Power Lifting is a major athletic event like weightlifting except for the method of lifting. It is very popular in many countries, especially India. The prize distribution commenced, and the Master of Ceremonies announced, "The silver medal goes to the first runner-up, Johny Thomas from India. Johny climbed onto the podium draped in the National Flag, received the Silver Medal, and the National Anthem played. It was a moment of pride and the result of months of hard work. He had done extremely well in the three types of lifts: squat, bench press, and deadlift. He had bettered his personal mark, which was a national record. He had given great competition to the winner and was just short of the mark for the Gold Medal.

There was a great celebration in the Indian Camp that evening, but the only thought on Johny's mind was to share the news with his parents. With his meagre pocket money, he went to the nearby booth and booked a call to his neighbour's house back in the village. It was not an era of mobile phones or direct telecasts. Although television sets had made their way to the Indian homes, his family didn't have one, and even if they did, the event wasn't being telecast live. Johny was still thinking of all the recent happenings when the operator's voice came through, "Sir, your call to Chalakudy in Kerala, India." Johny quickly asked his neighbour to call his dad or Mom. Since they were expecting a call from him, they hurriedly came over. Choked with emotions, he said, "*Appa*, (Dad) I've won the Silver medal." His parents were overjoyed and were rendered speechless. With great excitement, Johny narrated the events leading to his victory. All his parents could do was congratulate him, thank God, and wish him well. The call got cut as the operator said that the time was up.

There was a great celebration in their household that night. The whole locality got together, congratulating the parents and discussing the welcome of Johny. Back in his hotel room, Johny lay in bed wide awake, overwhelmed with emotions, and still processing all that went down, how his destiny had changed because of one single event.

About Six Years Before

It was the month of April. The results of the tenth grade had just come in. Though he had passed the exam, Johny hadn't done too well. He had just scraped through, and his dad wasn't very pleased about it. He gave him his piece of mind, leaving Johny disheartened. He stuck around his mother in the kitchen for the rest of the day, trying to avoid being in the presence of his father. His sisters tried to console him, saying that he could do better in the twelfth grade.

Meanwhile, his uncle, who had come over, told his dad, "Why

don't you let Johny come and stay with me for the summers? It could cheer him up and take his mind off his poor performance?" Johny stayed with his parents and eight siblings in a small village in Chalakudy, Kerala. His father worked in a factory as a supervisor and made barely enough money to look after his large family. Johny was one of the youngest and always had the love of his parents and elder siblings. That was one of the reasons why they overlooked his negligent attitude at school.

His uncle stayed at Trichur, another town not too far away. Johny's father pondered for a while about his brother's suggestion. He consulted his wife and decided that it was best to send Johny away to his uncle's place for the summers.

Johny was all excited about his holiday plans. On the bus, he asked his uncle what they were going to do. His uncle said, "We could go fishing, trekking through the jungles, maybe a little hunting, and if you behave well, maybe I could teach you how to drive the scooter." Johny was all too enthusiastic about the trip and remained on his best behaviour. His aunt and cousin sisters looked after him very well, and he had a great time.

He reminded his uncle about the scooter driving lessons. Sparing time from work, his uncle started giving him driving lessons. Time passed, and the summer vacation was almost over. One day when his uncle came home for lunch, he left the scooter keys on the scooter. Johny seeing the opportunity, slowly pushed the scooter onto the road, started it, and drove off. Hearing the sound, his uncle came out and called out to him to stop. Johny was not, however, able to control the scooter, and while taking a turn, he fell. Unfortunately, his right ankle came under the scooter, and he was grievously injured. His uncle came quickly, picked him up, and rushed him to the hospital. Though he had other minor injuries, his ankle injury was serious and needed immediate surgery as a tendon in the ankle was cut.

The surgery was carried out, and in a few days, he was discharged from the hospital. The wound also healed soon enough but left a deep scar and a visible limp that could not be avoided. His legs had also become weak due to the hospitalisation.

Father was unhappy and let it be known. He was also very angry with his younger brother for having introduced Johny to scooter driving. Johny's uncle was saddened by the whole turn of events. He didn't want his brother to be burdened by Johny's treatment. "Why don't I take Johny along with me?" He asked his brother. "Let him stay with us for some time and study at Trichur. The change of scene will probably do him good." Johny's Dad reluctantly agreed to the proposal, though his mom and sisters were not in favour of letting him go.

Johny was confused about the whole issue. He wanted to stay with his mom and siblings. However, he did not want to see his dad's sad face whenever he would see him limp. So, finally, it was decided, and Johny moved to Trichur with his uncle. There he continued with his schooling, treatment, and physiotherapy.

Before the present-day modern gymnasiums came into being, there were traditional gymnasiums that were very popular, especially in the State of Kerala. It was more of a hobby for people. The gymnasiums concentrated on bodybuilding and weightlifting. There were gymnasiums in all major cities and towns of Kerala in those days, with one very close to Johny's uncle's place. To improve his walking gait, on the suggestion of a friend, Johny's uncle enrolled him in the gymnasium. Johny quickly took a liking to the place and started working on his body. In no time, it became his favourite haunt, and he started spending all his spare time in the gymnasium. Since he was concentrating on physical fitness, his uncle encouraged him.

One day at the gymnasium, the coach asked him, "Why don't you take up bodybuilding? Since you are lightweight, there is less competition, and you could easily qualify for the tournaments."

Johny was enthusiastic about it, but his uncle was cautious. He said, "Let me speak to your dad."

Meanwhile, Johny had cleared his twelfth-grade exam, though not with very encouraging marks. It was going to be difficult for him to get admission to any college. He decided not to pursue studies and instead concentrate on bodybuilding. However, it was going to be a challenge getting his father to consent. His uncle remained the motivating factor and, along with his aunt, was key in convincing Johny's parents to allow him to pursue bodybuilding rather than joining up to learn a trade. Though his parents consented, they granted him only two years to train and perform in bodybuilding.

His coach was ecstatic and was sure that Johny had a great future. Johny worked very hard and, in no time, started participating in the 56Kg weight category of bodybuilding in various local championships. Soon, he was getting noticed at the local events and tournaments.

In a short time, he moved up the ladder and claimed the State Championship for bodybuilding. Now, his coach was convinced that he could do better and achieve greater heights. Since in the lower weights, bodybuilding was not very appealing to the public; he asked him to change over to Power Lifting. Johny took his coach's advice and continued training earnestly under the strict tutelage of his coach, who enrolled him in all possible competitions. In no time, Johny had become a popular contestant in all tournaments, and soon he won the State Championships in Power Lifting. He continued improving his score in every competition, and his family was eventually convinced that he was born an athlete and had a future in Power Lifting. Later, he went on to win the National Championships, breaking the National record in his weight category.

By this time, years had passed, and Johny was not the same frail boy in his teens. He had grown in figure, stature, and confidence. He was a bodybuilder, still winning prizes, as also the National record holder in his weight category for Power Lifting. It was the year of the World Games, in which the International Power Lifting Federation was holding the World Championship.

Johny was a natural choice to represent India. He travelled to attend the coaching camp. He trained well and was in a fit condition for the Championships. On the concluding day of the camp, the National Federation announced the selected team, and the President called individual players to his office. The President told Johny, "Johny, you know that there is not much support from the Government other than giving sanctions for the participation as also there are no sponsors for the event. The Federation is not very rich and cannot fully support the participants other than through payment of fees. I'm asking all players to deposit Rs two lakhs each to take care of the travel expenses and hotel stay. Only those players who can deposit the amount will be allowed to participate."

Johny was heartbroken. "Sir, you know that I come from a very poor family. They can barely afford to send me to participate in National events, let alone an International one. There is no way that I will be able to rustle up this much money," he said in a dejected tone. With hope, he added, "You have to help me. The President said, "I have tried out all my sources and could not shore up the required funds. This is a great opportunity for us to get noticed, but I'm not able to come up with a solution. He added, "Only those players who can deposit the money in time can be sent. There is no other way." Johny's eyes welled up with tears. He could only see darkness ahead of him.

Discouraged, he travelled back to Chalakudy and narrated the whole incident to his family. Despite all their discussions and brainstorming, they couldn't come up with a solution, and Johny decided to give up the idea.

Meanwhile, the news had spread in his village and in the regions around, all the way to his gymnasium in Trichur. Everyone was disappointed and saddened by the turn of events. As the final days approached, there was total gloom in the household. His uncle, who was his source of encouragement and support, was not willing to give up. He, along with the coach from the gymnasium, went around exploring various sources of funds. Finally, when nothing seemed to be working out, the people from around his locality in Trichur and his village in Chalakudy decided to contribute money and support him in his quest for glory. Once the decision was taken, in no time, voluntary donations were received from the villagers, and the required amount was deposited. Johny got the necessary sanctions, and the small team with a manager travelled all the way to South Africa for the World Championships.

*****

Event Day

The announcement by the Master of Ceremonies kept ringing in his mind "The silver medal for the first runner-up goes to Johny Thomas from India." With the National Anthem playing in the background, Johny's chest swelled up with pride. He was thinking of the difficult times, the frustrations, the challenges, and the sacrifices of his family, as also the contributions of all villagers that helped him get to where he was today. This medal was a tribute to all of them. He smiled, thanked God, and savoured the sweet taste of success seasoned with the salty tears streaming down his cheeks. All these years, he had focused on the silver lining of the dark clouds. His hard work, discipline, single-minded focus, and perseverance had paid off, and this was his moment of reckoning.

Postscript

Johny Thomas went on to participate in competitions for many years, and win many more medals for the nation, making his family and the country proud. He got employment in a public sector enterprise in the sports quota, continued as a member of their team, and in later years, became a mentor for their younger players.

This story has been inspired by the happenings in the life of a sportsperson and is a tribute to the resilience, hard work, and motivation of many other sportspersons who have been through similar circumstances and challenging times but persevered to emerge successful.

Untrodden Becomes Trodden

Kirti V

Unpredictable is the journey of life,
As we oft stand confused,
Whether our choice is right.

What seems untrodden for some,
Might be a cakewalk for others.
Who decides this? Can you guess?

The mind, the decision-maker,
Decides the path be taken,
Even if the heart differs.

Once her eyes are set,
The untrodden becomes trodden,
And life seems a breeze.

The breeze might encounter,
Many a hurdle as it blows,
And that makes it stronger than before.

Mysteries get unfurled,
And paths get clearer,
As the untrodden becomes trodden.

A Transition Unexpected!

Rita Som

My father was a central government employee. Those days and till he retired, the salary he drew was just enough to run the family with moderate luxuries. He didn't even live long to enjoy a pension like his colleague is enjoying, which would have been three times more than his salary due to the implementation of the 7th pay commission. Till recently, he showered his children with expensive gifts and once told me very proudly, "The pension I am drawing today is much more than the last salary I drew, and my own needs are very little now, so I can buy expensive gifts for my children and grandchildren and also giving them treats at the best restaurants."

His look and tone indicated a feeling of sympathy for me that my father didn't live long enough as a retired government servant to see these days of affluence…

Instead of feeling sad and dejected at this, my heart filled with adoration and admiration for my parents, who kept us always happy and satisfied. We never felt we were lacking in anything. I am very proud of them for giving us a very rich upbringing. Our house would be full of books. Some were bought for us on our birthdays or for scoring good marks in exams, and many we received as prizes for our academic achievements and other school achievements. In the sixties, we had a radio and a record player, and my father had the best collections of LPs and EPs.... He regularly spent a part of his salary on this, which many times annoyed my mother as she then had to manage a house of five members with only one breadwinner very stringently and wisely. I am sure that must have been a very difficult task for her. My father had very well-to-do friends who frequented our house more than us visiting theirs. People were attracted to my parents for their unusual warmth, simplicity, and positivity. There used to be laughter, listening to music, and discussion on politics and varied subjects over a cup of tea puffed rice, and fritters. So, we grew up in an enriching environment of good books, music, and wonderful people.

I have an elder sister and a brother younger than me.... many cribs for being the second of three children. Surprisingly I never did. This could be because of the way our parents treated and handled us devoid of disparity. School picnic, all three goes, or no one goes. Period. New dress all three get, or no one gets. Period. 'Period' word was not used at all those days, but their firm tone said it all and left no room for argument.

One big decision they had to make was about our further studies after graduation. This must have been the worst testing time they had to face in their entire life! There was hardly any age difference between us. We almost grew up together. All three of us went to school together and graduated from college one after the other. We both sisters chose Arts and our brother Science. It would be very difficult for our parents to provide professional courses to all three of us almost at one time. My father and mother, maybe after a lot of thinking and contemplation, decided that after graduation, all three of us would have to fend for ourselves! My elder sister, while she was in college, had started teaching in a school and continued even after she got married to an Army Officer, as wherever they were posted, the school principal's post would be hers due to her experience and qualification. I graduated the following year and married a businessman I was in love with, and eventually ventured into teaching. My brother took up a job with an MNC, and the company sent him to the US and sponsored his professional course in polyester staple fibre manufacturing, and today even after retirement, he is associated with many companies looking after their business development and quality.

All three of us became independent at a very early age since our parents made us fend for ourselves early, and we three reached such a pinnacle of success and achieved more but not less than our counterparts whose parents supported them for many more years financing their lives, their professional studies after graduation and, sponsoring their studies abroad. I am proud of my parents, who taught us to be independent, giving us exposure to good living and wonderful experiences, and, above all, did not ever give my brother special treatment since he was their 'male child'.

This upbringing helped me a lot later in my life when I chose a path less trodden. I spent forty years in the field of Education, managing a school, teaching in a college, setting up preschools and training teachers, which I still do, and finally retiring as a principal of a school. Life, as the saying goes, is unpredictable. The sudden death of my husband came as a bolt out of the blue, and my life turned topsy-turvy. I went blank about everything. Darkness and remorse engulfed me. After our daughter got married, it was only the two of us! I felt alone and wondered, 'How will I cope with the rest of my life without him?'

Like a zombie, I completed all the necessary rituals, after which all my relatives and friends went back to their routine life. My daughter stayed back by my side, and one day, she gave me the long-awaited news that I would be a grandma soon! I couldn't believe my ears! It is rightly said, "When God closes one door, he opens another one" …my happiness knew no bounds! This brought a 360* turn in my life. I gradually got control over myself and decided to take control over my life, too, as there was something to look forward to, and I could not afford to give my daughter a gloomy surrounding during her pregnancy.

On the other hand, the responsibilities of my late husband's engineering company needed my attention. All the unfinished projects that involved lots of money and commitment had to be completed. Everyone in the company looked up to me expectantly. I had no time to drown myself in sorrow. I had to take charge of things. But how would I do that? I was not an engineer and knew nothing about business. My transition from education into engineering and subsequently from an educationist to an entrepreneur happened like magic. This was possible only because of the wonderful people around me, my grit and determination, and the blessings of all up there in heaven. "Don't lose hope. You can do it. Take charge and carry on the legacy of this company," some good soul kept telling me. I mustered up the courage and took up the risk and challenge ahead of me. Thus, my journey as a woman in a male-dominated field of mechanical engineering started. With the help of my engineers, I completed all the unfinished projects. While doing that, more work started coming in. The company flourished. Today it is one of the best companies known for its superb engineering, manufacturing of fertilizer and chemical plant equipment for clients setting up plants in India and abroad.

People ask me that despite not having any previous knowledge and qualification, how could I cope in this male-dominated world of mechanical engineering. According to me major credit for this goes to my parents for their value-based upbringing, which was devoid of discrimination based on gender, which I mentioned earlier. I never felt different or less powerful than my male counterparts. They also ignited my hunger for knowledge in me by keeping us connected to books. Once I ventured into something new, I had to explore. I had to acquire knowledge about the equipment we manufactured and grasp the whole process of executing once we bagged the offer. At the age of sixty, I did not feel ashamed of learning from engineers who were much younger than me. The adage, 'Learning does not stop at any age,' was deeply imbibed in me. The day I stop learning will be my death. I was a quick learner too. Thus no one could fool me due to my lack of knowledge.

Common sense played a major role in my life. I have used it always and now to the fullest. I solved many problems using my common sense, and people around me thought I was very intelligent. My age was an advantage rather than a disadvantage. Several years of my past experiences made me wiser, and my mature brain grasped things faster.

Long years at school trained me to deal with people with patience. I excelled in people management. These attributes made me very confident, and in return, they helped my company to flourish.

With each passing day, I found myself getting more comfortable with my new-found work and with the people in this field. Eventually, the unknown, the untrodden path, became so much known to me that I started enjoying the world of mechanical engineering. Engineering, in fact, is so much a part of our day-to-day life! For all in our clan, all I can say is, "Stretch, stretch, Woman! Touch the Sky...Fathom the Ocean!

Mr. & Mrs. Robinson

Rupali Samant

A proud old tree stands tall with thicker branches,
Which are mostly covered with thick leaves,
Which Supports a nice big nest.
There are babies in them,
That no one can see except my family and me.
Right beside the nest stood the mother bird,

Being protective and looking lovingly
Her three young one's sleep like babies,
The father is seen guarding his nest with sheer pride.
The three babies are just a day old.
All the mother does is feed and feed them some more.
Fetching the food is a new game; in sync are they, as parents,
To bring in the feed, which ensures the family's happiness.
The babies are no longer new-borns,
They are young and robust, chirpy and fun fun fun.

I noticed they were trying to work their wings,
What a complete delight to see them do so
over and over again,
To only stop for their feed until the worms reach them.
From the loud sound of the mother bird, I assumed she
meant to say, "Stop it; it's too early to fly!"
Time flew by, and each day was a pleasure for me
to see them grow,

As a family of birds, I decided to name them 'The Robinsons.'
Mrs & Mr Robinsons and their young ones
Jack, James, and Jamie.
I realize how close and fine they are as a family.
Their nest is like a place where love and care reside.
Seasons are changing; the days and weeks go by,
Suddenly, one day I heard a lot of commotion coming from
the nest as I noticed.
While both the parents were not around.
The young ones started to get out of their home,
One by one, each sitting on the side of their nest,
Like curiosity kills the cat.
They had started peeking into the outside world,
All are eager to get out into the big bad world,
independent and free.

They're completely clueless about what life has to offer them,

What's the future for each of them separately?

Being unaware of their future, they feel excited and courageous about the ways forward in life.

While they feel positive, Mrs & Mr Robinson are taken aback,

As parents, they are hesitant, but they also feel sure in their hearts,

They knowingly recognized that this was the right time for Jack, James, and Jamie.

They certainly deserve their freedom.

They willingly together decide to support their first solo flight.

"Tomorrow's your big day," said the mother to her children,

"Rest well tonight; let's all eat, pray and huddle together for one last time."

"Remember a few things that I said to you today," as she glances at her husband and likes his reaction to continue to say,

"Never let fear come in your way.

Your mind has positively been made up to fly far, far away,

Opening your wings is simply taking the first bold step.

They are stronger and have enough strength than before to take the plunge to pursue your dreams."

"Make sure you do not knowingly hurt anyone in any way,
Do offer your help whenever required,
You must pray and tell the Lord each day,
Show thankfulness to God through Prayers."
Mr Robinson said, "Our home will never be the same
without you chit-chatters.
But the love and care for each other with always be there."
Mrs Robinson is happy to see her three children sleeping
together for the last time now.
She quietly snuggled next to her husband and let out a cry.
It sure seems like a gloomy and mournful place
to be in right now.
The next dawn brings along with it new hopes and desires,
The whole family gathers together to witness the wonderful
flight into the future.
Jack opens his wings and flies into the real world
in a blink of an eye,
He surely turns back and blows a few kisses to his parents,
While James and Jamie wave back,
As he flies higher and higher into the clear sky.
Bittersweet feelings consume the heavy hearts of the parents,
Memories Clog the minds of the siblings.
Mrs Robinson has to focus on her second son James,
He seems to appear timid, shy, and hesitant,

To be unable to do what his brother just did.

He takes his time, slowly but steadily, and he gathers the courage,

To move to the side of his home then flaps his wings twice,

To allow the wind to get under his wings,
which assists him in flying,

He finally flies high and happily moves towards his future without looking back.

The third and last child, Jamie, is their only daughter,

She's pampered and pretty but is the most attentive one
of the lots,

She follows instructions carefully. She first moves steadily
to the side of the nest,

Only after a good grip on her feet does she open her wings partially,

As she awaits patiently for the wind to give her the first lift in order for her to open her wings open fully.

She starts to fly from one branch to another,

Of the big old tree which hosts her nest.

She then turns around and flies back home to be with her parents for a wee bit,

And kisses them and says, "Thank you."

She warmly hugs them and makes sweet promises,

Of coming back home shortly.

She finally makes the flight with sheer confidence and joy.
Without the wind beneath her wings,
And whispers "goodbye!" to the lonely Robinsons.

Mrs & Mr Robinsons have kept themselves busy,
Unexpectedly one day, the whole family of five is back together,
And at times, they have gotten their sweethearts too.
The nest experiences life once again,
It feels like a lot of buzzing and humming.
As if someone is singing and the others are humming.
Since they are empty nesters, their social lives have changed.
They have started to visit folks or invite them over,
They sing together, play music too, make a lot of noise, and laughter surrounds them too,
To help fill the empty home with happiness.
They have accomplished things that they tick mark
on their buck list.
Presently, they are grandparents to Jack's children,
They feel a sense of joy and pride to see their children have found love and care.
And have started their own families.

Parents' love never fades away. Neither by time nor distance.
It continues to grow stronger and stronger as the days go by.
Our home will always be an empty nest.
That's where love, care, and happiness reside,
Do remember how nurturing your nest once was,
And as a mother, I hope you will crave it,
Cause the nest is always expecting you back home with new hopes and joy,
It's never gonna lose the love it has always had,
Cause that's your guiding light.

Autumn of Life

Col Arun Hariharan

Autumn was back again. Not that Ramesh Balmiki knew any fancy season names or had any romantic notions about any season as such. But what he detested about this season was the increased workload. With the lush green trees of Lutyens Delhi shedding leaves copiously, sweeping and clearing them was back-breaking work for him—a *safai karamchari* (sweeper) with the New Delhi Municipal Corporation (NDMC). His supervisor was quite a stickler too and would not give him duties regularly if he found any laxity in work. Hence, Ramesh busied himself and got on with the laborious task of clearing each dry leaf in his assigned area and collected them in a gunny sack. He muttered under his breath as he found another heap of dried leaves at the road bend. It was much larger than the usual conglomeration of leaves.

He started raking them in with his broom, when his broom hit something solid inside the leaves. He pushed the leaves aside to inspect.

His eyes widened in horror when he realized what was there inside the pile of leaves.

It was a newborn baby wrapped in a coarse cloth still with part of its umbilical cord intact. He stepped back in shock. He looked around furtively and then gathered the courage to check the child. The baby was alive but was burning with a fever and hence seemed to be in a stupor. Ramesh knew that he had to act now. He dropped his broom (the supervisor be damned) and gently picked up the child and rushed back home. Sunita, his wife gave him a questioning look when she opened the door of their squalid *jhuggi* (hutment) and saw him carrying a small baby in a dirty piece of cloth. He quickly explained her the happenings of the day, and both rushed to the Primary Health Centre (PHC) nearby.

The doctor in charge was a kindly old lady who knew Sunita well. Sunita had been trying to conceive for a while and had been unable to do so. The old doctor immediately cleaned up the child and began treatment. "Ramesh, you are a God send for this child. She'll be fine. If you had left her for some more time, she would have died either of exposure or some stray dog would have mauled her. Treat her as God's gift and the very child you both have been yearning for all this while" she told the couple.

*****

Vinita was as usual at the Qutub Plaza traffic signal in Gurgaon, late in the evening. It was a Friday, and the traffic was heavy. She was feeling very tired, not quite recovered from the viral she had last week. On top of that, the vehicular fumes were not helping her cause. But she strode from car to car clapping her hands and asking for money. Some of the commuters mockingly laughed at her garishly made-up face whilst some of the others cringed in fear. Emotions that were universally missing were that empathy and compassion. It had been a dusty September day and it was still warm. The trees around had shed their leaves and there was very little respite from the day's harsh sunlight. Most of the beggar urchins had scrammed for the night. She too was planning to head back to her squalid tin shed in the nearby slum after some time.

The signal had just turned red on the Faridabad Road and, the traffic coming from Delhi towards Gurgaon had just started moving. Suddenly, she heard the screech of brakes and a thud. She turned around with a jerk. She saw the rear end of a while SUV, which was apparently jumping the red light. The car stopped for a moment and then sped away. There was a commotion in the middle of the road junction. Vinita rushed to see what had happened. The car had hit one of the urchins, a scrawny tallish boy about eight or nine years of age. He appeared to be alive, but it seemed that one of his legs had been badly crushed by the car. The passers-by were of no help and after crowding around a bit and hefting the injured boy to the roadside, they slowly sauntered away. The boy was howling in pain. The police arrived, but then seeing that the victim was just a beggar boy and the car which had hit him had already fled, they lost interest immediately. Vinita realized she had to do something. She begged the cop to drop her and the boy to the nearest government hospital. The pot-bellied old patrolman reluctantly agreed and dropped her and the bleeding boy to the Gurgaon Government Hospital.

Luckily there was a doctor on duty in the hospital. He too gave Vinita a weird look. She just ignored him and asked him to quickly treat the boy. "I'll stabilize him, but it seems the bone is badly shattered, and we will need to operate to set it. But before that, I urgently need the consent of the child's parents."

Vinita realized, she did not know even the child's name, let alone his parents'. She gently spoke to the boy, who was now a little calmer since the doctor had probably given him a painkiller shot. "My name is Rashid. I don't have any parents. Both are dead," said the boy. At that moment, Vinita took a call. She signed her name on the parent consent form. The doctor raised an eyebrow on seeing it but said nothing thereafter and motioned the paramedic to prepare the boy.

*****

Sushma walked onto the stage, hand in hand, with a tall handsome man, who walked with a slight limp. They were the power couple of the moment and the toast of the city. Both were one of the youngest co-founders of a unicorn start-up in the Country. AUTO-MN was a disruptive idea right from the beginning. It was an app that gave an end-to-end solution to everything to do with automobiles-connecting the neighbourhood mechanic, spare part shop, car cleaner, etc to the end users offering a wide range of services including affordable yet reliable road-side-assistance. It had been a runaway hit right away. The couple was acclaimed TedX speakers too.

Sushma took the mic first. “Ladies and gentlemen, I would like you all to meet my wonderful parents—Ramesh and Sunita, because of who I am and what I am today” Ramesh and Sunita were escorted onto the stage as the spotlight focussed on them. The hall broke into a thunderous ovation.

Sushma continued “People say autumn is the season when leaves fall from trees and everything turns brown and drab, but for a little abandoned baby many years ago—it was a season of hope, of finding loving parents and of life.”

Her tall partner then took the mic. “I am the luckiest person in the world. For I have a father and mother rolled into one. The strongest person I know, who again on an autumn night many years ago ...gave life to a beggar boy who lay dying all alone in the world and then brought me up against all odds.”

The spotlight focussed on an ageing but elegant transgender as she walked up the stage, again to rapturous applause. Rashid bowed down and touched her feet before hugging her, choked with emotions.

Our Lives, Our Rules

Ishita Sharma

Want to live our life on our rules and regulations,
Want to live our life like independent creatures.

Society will curtail our freedom,
so, the need is to struggle.
People will judge us on their terms
so, the need is to change their mindset.

The ancient perceptions should be broken now,
The prejudice that we are weak should be changed now.
This is the time to make everyone understand that we don't need support but some cooperation.

Now, we have to be bolder enough to fight the world
and societal constraints.
Now, we have to take the initiative to get our constitutionally
granted freedom.

People have to understand that we are not weak
People have to realize the freedom that we seek.

Live Your Dream

Vivek Gulati

One humid evening, Vijay was sitting on his father's rocking chair in his luxurious penthouse in Mumbai; gazing at the trophies he had won in the past five years. A reel of his past was playing on a loop in his mind, and he was feeling restless. He got up, and after pouring himself a stiff peg of Glenlivet 12, stood by the huge window looking over at the grand view of the Arabian Sea.

Vijay was born into a family of scholars. Both his parents were senior lecturers at a renowned college in Delhi and his elder sister was an intern at a premier medical college. His parents, and by extension his entire family, had very high expectations from him. Though Vijay had excelled in all the subjects since school, his heart was elsewhere, and he dreamed of excelling on the silver screen. A good observer, he was addicted to the stage and was mostly found around the stage rather than the classrooms, helping others with their roles or just soaking in the creative atmosphere backstage.

To uphold family traditions, the ever-obedient son got admission to IIM, Ahmedabad, and to no one's surprise, was hand-picked by India's biggest advertising agency as an Executive for Strategy and Planning.

Since Vijay possessed a very analytical mind and was a great believer in research-based decisions, he made his mark even among the ocean of employees working at the big agency. His understanding of briefs and the contents of presentations was superior to his peers, but he was unable to rise in the hierarchy because of his handicap—his stutter. He used to stammer since birth, so his best written PPTs were presented by others, corporate power-hungry vultures who gobbled up all the credit. Due to his inability to present, Vijay was left with doing research and writing presentations.

Soon frustration got the best of him, and he became depressed as he realized that if he is not allowed to make presentations because of his handicap, how will he realize his dreams of making it in the industry? But fate had different things in store for him. One time, he was at a product shoot for a new bike his agency was launching. Since the client's Head of Marketing was coming, he had been instructed to attend the shoot by his manager.

While the male and female models were posing with the bike, Vijay stood in the corner smoking. The photographer, a very big name in the industry, was increasingly getting irritated as he could not get satisfactory results even though almost half the day was over.

The client sensed the situation and wildly called for Vijay. "What are you doing here smoking like an engine while my time and money are being wasted? Have you bothered to check the shoot results?" he yelled at Vijay. Continuing the barrage of Punjabi expletives, he said "Just get the shoot sorted, or else I will sack the agency." Vijay panicked and rushed to the photographer to try to handle the situation. The photographer was one hell of an arrogant person and wouldn't give a clear answer. "The male model is worse than a cupboard" was all he kept screaming angrily. Immediately Sapna, the assistant director, took Vijay aside and told him that the boss is furious because of the lack of expressions from the 'cupboard' male model. Handling two large egos in a heated atmosphere was not easy for Vijay and operating in crisis mode, he implored Sapna and pleaded with her to help salvage the situation, fearing that he would be fired if the client sacked the agency. Sapna was surprised that a good professional like Vijay was feeling insecure and thought to help him as she had always secretly admired his good looks and felt bad when people laughed at him whenever he tried making a lengthy conversation.

She went to the photographer, who had stormed off set for lunch and was grumpily talking to the client. Sapna stood beside them and when she thought that both were thinking to pack up, she nonchalantly remarked: “Can’t we try another model?” This was the last straw for the photographer who got really mad at her and yelled, “Do you even know what you are talking about? We have already wasted half a day and now we should start another exercise of scouting for another model. Do you think I sit idle? I don’t have any dates to spare this month…,” he went on and on.

The client looked at Sapna and said, “Were you just casually making a remark or do you have a real solution?” Sapna nodded, “Yes, I have a solution, and here is our male model” and shoved Vijay in front of the two men. For a moment, there was a pin-drop silence and a wave of total shock and disbelief clouded both of their faces. After sizing up Vijay over and again, the photographer said, “let’s give it a try” and excitedly waved towards his crew. That was the last that was heard of the ‘cupboard’ male model on that set.

The stars aligned, and after a few trial shots the ace photographer ran towards the client triumphantly and hugged him “Yes, we have got it, this one’s a winner.” They both saw the preview and the campaign was approved in a few days’ time. The bike became a rage with the youth and so did Vijay. He was soon flooded with modelling offers from major brands and taking that as a sign, he left his job and moved to Mumbai—the City of Dreams.

He flourished, and on a particularly busy weekend shooting for a suiting ad in Hyderabad, he received a frantic call from his coordinator. A big movie director had seen his ad on TV and wanted to sign him for his forthcoming venture, where he was launching the daughter of a reigning Bollywood superstar.

Vijay could sense the excitement in his voice, but cut him short and told him "You know my shortcoming, how can I become a movie star?" Bala, a well-known casting Director, said "Just meet him once, maybe God has made some plans for you." Vijay called the big showman from Hyderabad and said, "Sir, I am honoured by your offer, but I would like to tell you upfront that I have an issue with my speech. I stammer even when I have to say a long sentence and struggle to get the words out." The big man heard him patiently and told him to meet him anyway.

On reaching back to Mumbai, Vijay was picked up by Bala from the airport and they drove straight to Red Chilies' special effects studios where the director was giving finishing touches to his now complete film.

The director met Vijay warmly and said, "I am impressed not only by your personality but also by your honesty." He then offered Vijay to join him as an Assistant Director and learn the ropes of filmmaking. "It's not necessary that you can only make a mark in front of the camera, there are many other behind the scenes options that can help make you a big man in the film industry. You just need to have passion, focus, and God's blessings to take you to the top. Will you dare to choose the path untrodden?" These words were music to Vijay's ears. Everything clicked into place, and at that moment, the ace Director looked like God to him. He immediately said 'YES', and in what was the biggest gamble of his life, left his flourishing modelling career.

He soon realized that what he mistook as a zeal for acting, was for cinema itself. The passion for the stage had burned within Vijay since childhood, and he grabbed this opportunity with both his hands. He worked tirelessly and within a short period of time, everyone could sense that they were nurturing a great talent. Vijay learnt all the ropes of filmmaking from the legendary director, be it scripting, photography, direction, or editing, and even accompanied him to the song recordings. Combining his analytical prowess with the subject closest to his heart, Vijay exceeded all expectations and was soon launched as an independent director by his mentor. As it was, the movie proved to be the biggest hit under the showman's banner.

From there, his career only grew, and Vijay started getting multiple offers from other production houses, but he proved his loyalty by sticking with his mentor. Everything he touched turned to gold, and every venture was not only commercially successful but also won critical acclaim in India and globally. He started writing books about filmmaking and giving lectures in various filmmaking and acting institutes.

In a glowing tribute at the last award show, the showman had said "Vijay is the perfect example of someone who believed in himself and followed his passion. He overcame his handicap and proved to the world that a powerhouse talent cannot be kept away from success for long if he is ready to risk everything to pursue his passion." As Vijay accepted the trophy from him, he bowed down to touch his feet. Misty eyed, he looked over at him and proudly announced, "There are more talented people than me and they need the hand of God to become as successful as me, my life took a huge turn after I met Sir."

As Vijay stood at the window, looking at the waves gently crashing on the shore, he couldn't help but think of the showman. He thought back to the time when he believed his handicap was a limitation, and how the director's words changed his life. It is true that one only needs the guiding eye of a mentor to achieve impossible heights. Draining the last of his drink, Vijay smiled and thanked the stars for sending him the one who gave him the courage to follow his dreams.

Eyes on Me

Praneel Dev

Eyes are looking, judging, and watching,
Their staring leaves my heartbeat jumping.
They want all of me to be put on display,
And then to pick my path without my say.

To all their big schemes, I say nay,
I'm plotting my course my own way.
I want them to come tag along and see,
As I build my own tower taller than a redwood tree.

I'll rule my own castle and live in it free,
So that when all is done, I can say with glee,
To all those looks, stares, and judgements,
I looked past you and still built my settlements.

Confidence and belief were my instruments,
On them, I played a tune, accomplishments.
And now, I look back years with ears ringing,
All eyes were on me, and I left them applauding.

A Beautiful Beginning

Mehak Lakhwani

Amu was sitting in a pool of blood! She had just sliced her palm brutally near the thumb and was horrified at the sight of it. She had done it on a whim and had not realized that it would be so severe. Her younger sister was clearing up the blood frantically off the floor while Amu looked devastated and was thinking, 'What would her mother say?' Dazed, she sat on the floor kneeling, bracing her hand, sprawled on the floor, waiting, and imagining her mother entering the room in fury, dizzy to face her wrath!

Amu was a beautiful girl for her age and that was exactly why she had a lot of attention coming her way in school. Boys used to come after her, make prank calls at her home, and always try to catch her attention in some or the other way. Amu was a bright girl; she was very creative, she painted well, she could dance beautifully, she was also fond of reading, she was an athlete too and teachers loved her. But all the unwanted attention that she got from the boys became a cause of a bitter relationship between Amu and her mother. Her mother, like most mothers, never thought her daughter was good enough or innocent enough and always blamed Amu for all the nuisance the boys created in her life. This not only stressed Amu but also became the cause of her grief. She secretly wished many times if only she could disappear somewhere and not be seen.

She spent all her school life in pain and suffering because her mother firmly believed that her daughter would somehow be defiled because of her reckless manners and easy happy nature. Fearing imaginary shame Amu would bring to the family by her very being, she beat her up every day, cursed her, and gaslighted her.

As expected, Amu lived in fear and was terribly unhappy. For the life of her, she could not understand what her fault was as she saw many girls around her as friendly as she was with the opposite sex. Amu had started believing that whatever wrong happened in her life was her own fault and that she was in fact not a good girl and she kept wondering in the wee hours of the night (most nights were spent awake) why she was like that.

Today too, her mother had ranted and raved at Amu for being Amu. She had accused her of things a mother should never say to her teenage daughter; she had verbalized and abused her and said words that could scar her fragile mind for the rest of her life. Unable to bear the pain Amu had thought of harming herself, not sure if she wanted to kill herself or just wanted her mother's sympathy for once. She couldn't take the insult and humiliation anymore but being only sixteen she couldn't figure out a way to escape the agony.

"Mumma, do you love me at all?" a very pained Amu had asked her mother only a few minutes back. To which her mother had stared at her coldly with sheer disgust and left the room. The picture of her mother's face full of revulsion against her, had left her heartbroken and sad. What had she done ever for her mother to hate her so much? Why was her mother always finding fault in her behaviour? Why did she not like her? With these questions swirling in her mind, Amu without thinking, as if on remote and before it could register what she was doing, had slit her hand.

And crying in pain and fear, she wasn't sure if this would arouse pity in her mother for her or simply more anger.

She was right. It had only infuriated her more.

*****

Now…

Amu has been married for eighteen years now and was preparing dinner for her husband. Her husband, a businessman, had no time for her; and if he did love her, he had no time to show that love. Life was just the usual grind. Her daughter, Renee, sixteen years of age, (almost the same age as Amu, when Amu had tried to end her life) sitting on the kitchen counter had asked her something about her childhood and Amu had opened up about that horrific incident to someone in years and that too to her daughter. Renee was tearing up at her mother's story and was completely in shock, she was finding it hard to believe that her loving grandmother, who always showered her with love and whom she loved so much, had been this extreme person at one point in time.

She could understand what Renee was going through. Isn't it a very strange type of grief, to come to know that your doting grandparents were once bad parents?

But nevertheless, one thing Amu couldn't deny was that her mother was a loving grandmother. It was odd that she would advise Amu, who was a mother to a teenager now, to go easy on Renee's tantrums and understand that this was an age where she would naturally be attracted to boys! She sometimes almost laughed out loud at the irony of it all.

"Mumma, I can't believe *nani* (grandmother) was like this to you!" Renee sobbed.

"Don't worry Mumma, when I go to college and start earning, I will take you with me" Renee whispered to her mother, fighting back her tears.

Amu for the first time felt a sense of relief that someone had spoken in her favour and understood her pain. Although guilt was still biting her for ratting out on her mother, today she wanted her daughter to know a part of her life that she had kept under wraps for so many years. Amu was the type of person who did not like to share her pain because telling it to someone meant going through it all over again. Her daughter who loved her dearly was completely stunned and was numbed over hearing her mother's story.

"Mumma, is that why *Nani* got you married so early and didn't let you study?"

"I don't know my love, maybe it was my destiny. I, for the life of me, still haven't been able to figure out why she behaved as she did. I don't know what insecurity or something else drove her to be like that with me" she sighed. But it's in the past now. My only regret is that I couldn't study further. I was a bright child, I wanted to do a Ph.D."

Amu was feeling exhausted from the whole episode of recalling the hurt in the past and was feeling drained when her husband walked into the house. As usual, preoccupied with himself, he stomped his feet, consumed by his own thoughts and frustration with the business and the day he had gone through.

Amu wanted to calm him down, but she knew it was a futile effort; had been for many years! She also knew his answer if she asked him the cause of his frustration. "You women won't understand a thing! And this is none of your business!" This had become quite a routine now.

Amu quietly retreated to the kitchen and waited for her husband to freshen up and come for dinner.

Subdued for so long in her life, Amu had forgotten that she had a voice and that she was an independent human being. Her whole life she had been dictated around and she only knew that way of living. She loved her daughter dearly and so did Renee. Since the moment she had had Renee, she had decided to be the most loving and understanding mother to her daughter and be that mother whom she could never have.

Recently her husband's aggression had taken a toll on her mental health. All the down talking, and his rude demeanour had been very taxing on her mind and self-esteem. Though Amu was a homemaker, she had never stopped educating herself. Her instinct to learn and read more and more had not only multiplied with time, but also her thirst for how women empowered their life and lived a fulfilled life had found a place in her heart and mind. She had also found a group of like-minded women and their insightful and meaningful conversions lit up her soul. Slowly but surely, she was changing, coming into herself, and was inclined towards better things in life.

All of this was keeping Amu sane and thinking. In her case, knowledge was truly powerful. Amu did everything dutifully and with complete responsibility but somewhere in her heart, she remained aloof from all the bickering around her. The fact that Renee was leaving in just a few days for her higher studies was gnawing at her. How would she spend her days then? The futility of her life was mounting high up and it looked like an endless road where she did not have a partner to accompany and unfortunately no destination either!

The day finally arrived which was as dreaded as was awaited! Renee was all packed to leave to pursue her dreams. This was one of Amu's achievements! She had pushed and persuaded her husband to let Renee go out to pursue higher education. So, it was also a reason why Amu had a feeling of accomplishment, that despite all the odds she had been able to pave the way for her daughter. With unshed tears in her eyes, she managed to bid goodbye to the light of her life.

Days had passed since Renee had left for law school in London. Amu was not a clingy mother but evermore she started avoiding Renee's calls. She would get on a call and then immediately excuse herself. She tried to interact with her as little as possible. Renee often called and texted, but it wasn't enough! Amu missed her and avoiding her was like a defence mechanism that helped her shield her awry emotions. She engrossed herself in reading more than ever. She also joined a book club and tried to keep herself busy. She was all by herself now.

One night Amu was feeling very anxious while serving dinner to her husband because she wanted to talk about something important and she did not know how he would react.

"I went to the Edu brain institute today" Amu broke the silence abruptly.

"Why?" Her husband asked nonchalantly without looking up from his plate.

Hesitantly Amu answered, "I was thinking since Renee has also gone now and you are so occupied with your work, I just thought I would pick up teaching…"

"And What happened?"

"They asked me when I could join…"

Pause.

"How much are they giving you?"

With her heart hammering inside her, she replied, "Fifteen thousand, I think… I didn't clearly talk about that since I wasn't sure if you would allow me to do it."

"Huh? That's what I give to the boy who cleans my counters!"

"Ha ha ha!"

Amu turned red with a feeling she couldn't decipher humiliation or indignation.

It flared her up and she lost it right in that moment! Everything that had been bottled up for so long just gushed out with a force and exploded out of her.

"This! Exactly this attitude that you have! This shows the respect you have for me, I don't know about love because you are never there for moments of love. I've spent eighteen years of my life and marriage only waiting for you! Trying to believe that I'm here because you love me… but not now....” she fumed.

It isn't love if you don't ever show it! Love needs to be expressed, it needs to be felt, and it needs to be spoken!!

I am so tired of being the understanding wife all the time, but you don't have any time for me, that you have been never there when I needed you. Even today. Do you have any idea of how much I miss Renee? How do I fill my empty days? How do I spend my time when you are out making deals? I never cribbed because I thought, someday you will understand, someday you will support me, but I was wrong. You will never change. If I don't take hold of my life now, I will die a lonely old woman, which I don't want to and will not let happen.

It's your turn now! Either you change or I am leaving you. “She continued, “I will inform Renee; maybe go to her, maybe just live alone…I don't know, but what I do know is that I'll leave early tomorrow. How I wish things had been different. I never wanted much, just a little bit of your time and understanding. But no! You have never ever understood.” Have a busy, happy life!”

With that final stroke, Amu turned with a flourish and left her husband stunned and speechless on the table staring after her in disbelief!

Florescence in Eternity

Ramya V

The fiery red ball was slowly sinking into dark slumber. It was celebration time in the Sethupathy household. Hundreds of guests were gathered to congratulate Yazhini for bagging the gold medal in her post-graduation. Her mother Savithri was busy monitoring the overall arrangements.

"Cheers!" Sethupathy and his close circle of friends were discussing his precious moment.

"So, what is next Sethupathy? Which hospital have you chosen for her to join as an Orthopaedic surgeon?" one of them raised the question.

"Yazhini is his only daughter. She has made him proud today. Who knows, he might build a new hospital for her. What say granite business magnet Sethupathy?" another commented, and the rest continued laughing.

Indeed, Sethupathy was one of the top ten businessmen in India with his granite trade flourishing across borders. His son Mithran completed his business administration and had been working with his dad for the past four years. Some day in the distant future he would be taking over from his father.

"I and Savithri wished to see Yazhini as a doctor. Our vision has come true today. I will leave her with the choice of choosing the hospital she wants to join. Already from today morning, I am receiving so many phone calls from the deans of the hospital in other cities too requesting her to join in theirs." Sethupathy was flaunting his proud moment.

The same was the situation with Savithri and her friends and relatives. She elaborated on Yazhini s intelligence right from her childhood where she not only always stood first in her class but also how she aced the board exams and entered the medical college on a merit basis.

"One missed call is enough from her father to obtain a medical seat in any of the top colleges in our city. But we are so blessed that Yazhini's marks itself fetched her admission," Savithri continued her pompous speech.

As the discussion about Yazhini went on, the girl in place stood in a corner with folded hands. Though born and brought up in riches, Yazhini chose to be simple in her needs and so were her thoughts. She felt contended in achieving her parent's dream. So far, she had walked on the path shown by them. Only she knew that her future steps would be purely her decision and it would be tough for her to convince her parents. Yet, she was determined to take the road less travelled.

A few days went by with happiness spreading over every second. That evening Yazhini was deeply buried inside her laptop and Sethupathy had some leisure time that he wanted to spend at home.

"What is it dear? You haven't said which hospital you would like to join?" caressing her hair gently, her father inquired.

"Dad, I have decided to work in Maelagrammam*." Without any expressions Yazhini replied.

"What?" Savithri dropped her 20k worth of coffee mug on the floor.

"Mom! Why did you get so worked up? I think it is a prank, right Yazhini?" Mithran joined in the conversation.

Before Yazhini could answer, Savithri replied in a serious tone.

"Mithran, you know she isn't the playful type."

A deep silence prevailed. All of them were analysing the name Yazhini had mentioned. It was a remote village situated in the southern tip of Tamil Nādu. The name was well known to many as most of the population included the tribal community. Though the place had major facilities, it was still considered to be backward in the social economic status. Sethupathy couldn't even believe that his daughter, a multimillionaire would utter such a name.

"Now I get it. Yazhini I understand you plan to spend some time in social service, right? Dad, your daughter is only making you proud even more. We can buy an estate nearby for her stay and I shall take care of all the arrangements. Maybe for a few months, she can stay there, and she would become famous worldwide." Mithran broke the calmness.

Savithri knew about her daughter. She did not consider any truth behind Mithran's words.

"Yazhini, speak up!" Savithri commanded as she was losing patience.

Yazhini stood from the couch.

"Dad, Mom, I am serious. I have already opted to work in the Maelagrammam Government Hospital as an Assistant Orthopaedic surgeon. And Mithran! It is not for any kind of stunt or drama as you imagine. I have planned to stay there for some years."

Sethupathy was shocked hearing his daughter talk this way. At the same time, he did not want to turn harsh on her.

"Yazhini, though you are younger than Mithran, I have always known you were more mature than him and it has been quite evident in your activities. If you have taken such a hard decision I know there is some reason behind it. You have my approval on one condition. You shouldn't be staying in the allocated quarters. As Mithran said, your stay and transportation would be under my supervision."

Yazhini was pleased and she ran to her dad. Her tears fell on his shoulder. He gently patted her.

Like the forest fire, the news ran through each of the households in Mealagrammam (Fictional Name) and its neighbouring villages. In a few days, Yazhini was settled in her new place. She took care of the morning O/P (Outpatient) schedule, and the afternoons were in her department. Her colleagues informed her that they do not get many patients every day as the people were known to treat themselves using the herbs and medicinal plants that grow on the pathway leading to the hills. Sometimes when they don't find the needed plants they rush here at the last minute. Yazhini observed it was quite true. In the coming days, the usual trend began to change.

With her gentle smile and friendly nature, she won the hearts of the little children.

A five-year-old boy came in the morning with a high temperature.

"Hello! What is your name?"

"Velan" his mother answered on his behalf.

"What did you do Mr. Naughty? Your temperature is 102."

He was half sleepy in his mother's arms but managed to smile at Yazhini. She continued her conversation and his mother kept gazing at them both.

"Nothing to worry about, just a viral infection. It will settle in two days. Velan you should take your medicines on time. Only then you can go to school soon, okay?"

"*Akka* (elder sister), I don't go to school."

Yazhini stood from her chair and neared him.

"Why Velan? You don't like to study? What will you do after you become a big boy?"

"I will cut wood like my father."

This was not the first time she heard something like this. Most of the kids whom she has been seeing here weren't interested in going to school though the Government school provides free education along with mid-day meals.

"Thanks, Doctor Akka," Velan's mother joined her palms together and walked out. Yazhini's name had indeed become, 'Doctor Akka' to those visiting the hospital, and that made her famous in a short period.

Though not ill, still few women frequented the hospital just to have a friendly conversation with Yazhini. They liked her down-to-earth nature which led to having a close set of friends. Thilaga, a twenty-year-old girl was one among them and she was even close to Yazhini. Even Yazhini loved the company of this talkative girl.

One fine evening Thilaga invited Yazhini to their village deity's temple. She elaborated on their festivals and requested Yazhini also to participate in the upcoming ones. Together they travelled through the mountains and Yazhini was happy viewing the beautiful lands and serene scenery.

"Thilaga, I wanted to ask you for a long time."

"Tell me Doctor Akka."

"Why are the kids not attending school?"

Thilaga burst into laughter.

"Doctor Akka, our kids are scared. They find it difficult to study. What are we going to do after studying? Stay here, get married, and settle with kids, for this why should we burden ourselves? There is plenty of ways to earn our living here."

"Have not even one person thought to become a doctor or take some other profession?"

"A few do study and move to the city. I am not interested in it, Doctor Akka. I want to stay at home, help my mother, play with my friends, and enjoy life," she said with innocence in her words.

The thought about the kids' education kept disturbing Yazhini's mind. So, on the weekends, in her free time, she planned to take special classes for the kids. The word spread throughout the village through Thilaga. Soon a few kids came to her house. Yazhini made arrangements in her garden. Initially, two to three kids came forward. Seeing the way, she taught them more kids soon joined in. Their parents were surprised to see their kids learn so much.

Later she visited one of the kid's households to meet his parents. They welcomed her with much happiness.

"Doctor Akka, my daughter is now speaking a lot. She is writing something on the floor and says it is my name. I am so happy. Thank you, Doctor Akka."

Seeing Yazhini, many came to meet her.

"Your kids are very intelligent by nature. It is time to send them to school so that they can learn more. How long do you all want them to stay here? There are so many professions to choose from. Please do not confine them inside this place. This place will always remain your homeland but at the same time, your kids' future is important as well. Let them go to the neighbouring towns for higher studies. If ever you want any kind of help I am always reachable. Please remember that and I request you all once again to continuously send your children to school." Yazhini said wholeheartedly.

All were surprised by her speech. The village Chief came forward.

"What she says is true. We have to take the step to make our children's life better." He turned towards Yazhini.

"Dear, you are so kind. God bless you."

Yazhini did not stop there. Every day she ensured the kids went to school and connected with the school Principal on the status.

Sethupathy and Savithri had been watching their daughter through the installed CCTV cameras. Since it had been long, they travelled to meet her.

It was late in the evening and Yazhini was surprised to see her parents. She ran to them and hugged them close.

"So how is my 'Doctor Akka' doing?" Sethupathy smiled at her.

"Dad!" she slightly sulked.

"Yazhini, isn't this social service?" Savithri asked raising her eyebrows.

"Mom!"

"Savithri, first let her freshen up."

In some time, they gathered for dinner.

"Mom, as you or Mithran may feel this is not any service. Do you remember my school trip in my tenth grade?"

Savithri and Sethupathy exchanged confused looks.

"We had gone to Kanyakumari for a week. During boating, our biology teacher was explaining about the water plants. Though our teachers instructed us not to step into the water a few of them were curious and walked near the shore stepping into the cold water. Suddenly blood was oozing out from their legs. They panicked and screamed though they never felt any pain. When looked closely, we found it to be leeches clinging to their skin and sucking their blood. Even after removing them, the blood flow couldn't be stopped. Hearing their screams a few people came to the rescue. We learned they belong to the local tribes. A few women ran and came back in a jiffy with different kinds of leaves. They smashed it using a stone and applied the paste on the legs. In no time the blood stopped. They also advised them to stay for a while and then leave the place. I had a conversation with them. I understood not just leeches they knew medicinal plants even for wild insect bites. I was surprised but what shocked me was that they never knew the name of the plants. They could identify the variety by its structure and knew the combination to treat some allergies and rashes. They felt there wasn't much need to exactly know the name which took me by storm."

Her parents were listening carefully to each of her words. Savithri remembered the trip, but she hadn't paid attention to it then.

"Dad, after having interacted with them over these months I well understood they are brilliant in their own ways. With the right education, they can also enter various fields and achieve big. It is not that they aren't aware of all these. A few of them do emerge but I feel their entire clan needs to rise. In the coming years, we should be able to see them everywhere. Just a little step from my end and if a seed blooms from my efforts, I would feel contended."

Sethupathy looked deeply at Yazhini. Is it his little princess talking with so much social responsibility? He was amazed at her thoughts and intense intentions.

"How long do you want to stay here Yazhini?" Savithri questioned her.

"I have fulfilled your dream of becoming a doctor. Now I am fulfilling the goal that intruded on me during my school time. Please, Dad, let me continue to be here for some more time."

"Yazhini. I have always been proud of you and still, I am. You can stay here however long you want."

"But?" Savithri interrupted.

Sethupathy stopped her.

"Savithri, everyone has goals and ambitions in life, and they struggle to achieve them. The world wants to see only the result of whether they have reached there or not. Nobody bothers about the path they have taken and the struggles in it. Our daughter gives importance to the path as well though it is not a usual one. We should support her as parents."

Yazhini rested on her dad's shoulder with silent tears spilling over. Savithri also noticed her husband's moist eyes.

Fruits of Hard work

Anthony Fernandes

People teased and laughed at me,
because I didn't own a vehicle.
I decided what I should be,
without even owning a cycle.

Nobody feeds me,
Neither do they bother.
I knew how to be,
as great as my mother.

Ignoring the worldly gossip,
I carried on with my plantation.
In spite of financial hardships,
I never lost determination.

Now the world sees me differently,
They don't see what I don't own.
As I always was friendly,
I am now enjoying the fruits of the trees I have grown.

Crossroads

Monika Patel

As the crowds cheered and clapped for Viraj Mehta, his eyes were searching for her. He was asked to address the gathering; after all, he was being honoured with the "Innovative Farmer" Award. He had won the prestigious award at the young age of forty. As he stood up to speak he kept looking for Deepa, and there she was. Seeing her at the award function meant everything to him. As he began his acceptance speech, the past decade of his life sped before him like the turn of a kaleidoscope. Coming back to the present he delivered his short speech to another round of applause. He wanted to be away from the crowds and go and be with his family and his beloved wife.

He was just stepping down the dais when one of his friends asked him to speak about his achievements to a newspaper journalist and appear for an interview with a TV channel. He immediately gave his assent and told her to fix an appointment right away. He wanted to savour the moments of accomplishment and joy with his friends and kin.

Sandhya Deshmukh was a journalist for a leading English daily and a meeting was fixed for that very evening. He was glad that he was in Pune for the function or else she would have had to travel to Satara where Viraj lived and practiced organic farming. IITian farming in some obscure village yet managing to stand out from the crowds. He knew this curiosity factor about him was what interested journalists the most; Sandhya being a point in case.

Many heads turned as he walked into the hotel lobby for the interview. He was tall, his fair face was tanned from working in the sun. His hair was styled, and his eyes were hidden behind branded sunglasses. His attire in no way revealed his profession. He was aware of his good looks which showed in his confident strides. Sandhya thought his pictures didn't do justice to him as she stood up to approach him. He looked like a model, and he should have been a model at least if not an actor, certainly not a farmer, innovative or otherwise; Sandhya thought to herself, as she waited for him to join her on the couch. She couldn't wait to find out how this engineer turned to farming.

After the formalities, they settled down for the interview. Sandhya began in her usual style. She always encouraged her subjects to tell their stories in their own words.

Rarely interrupting, nudging when needed but never intruding in their thought process. Viraj seemed ill at ease initially, hesitant on how to begin but settled down quickly and the flow of talk was relaxed.

"Congratulations first of all for your achievement," began Sandhya.

"Thank you! and thank you for inviting me for this interaction. I am grateful to your publication for giving me this opportunity. I hope my story inspires at least some young people to follow my way of life."

"So, let's begin from the beginning. .... your childhood days?" nudged Sandhya.

"Well, growing up in Pune was culturally and academically enriching. My father was a banker, and my mother was a high school mathematics teacher. My paternal grandmother stayed with us in

Pune till I was ten years old to look after me as both my parents worked full-time. My grandfather lived in our native place Satara. His passion was his farm, he refused to stay away from farming and his land. I would spend most of my holidays with my grandfather on the farm. From a very young age, I was exposed to various techniques of farming and rural life. Hard work and dedication to passion were all around me. My grandmother made sure I was exposed to both Marathi and English literature. She used to read to me every day. After I was old enough to let myself in the house, eat by myself and do my homework and studies, my grandmother went back to be with my grandfather in their village. Both my grandparents instilled the value of hard work in me. Throughout my high-school days, I participated in multiple extracurricular activities, be it dramatics, singing, or debate and recitation competitions. They helped me become a confident person, capable of articulating my thoughts into action. To get up at 5 am, study for an hour then go and swim in the public pool which was a stone's throw away from our house was my early morning routine."

"In my teenage years, I was consumed by the computer revolution. I decided very early in my teens to work in the field of computer engineering. With support and help from my parents and lifelong values of hard work instilled in me, I cracked the IIT entrance with flying colours."

"I remember vividly," continued Viraj "just before I joined the college in Mumbai I visited my grandparents' farm. They were aging but their zeal and dedication were still the same. My only worry was who will look after the farm after my grandparents? I did not want the land to be sold off ever or even given for cultivation to some strangers. I always was and still am very attached to the farmland"." While at college I visited Satara as often as I could. Somehow the connection was so strong that it brought me back to it permanently, after a decade."

Sandhya probed "Then what about your engineering?"

"Everything was a cliché...... I completed my graduation and like every software engineer got a job paying handsomely, in the US. After living there for three years my family found me a life partner. My life was scripted like most IITians who live abroad-well paid jobs, partners from similar backgrounds and professions, and are as committed to work as me. As years passed I grew professionally and so did my wife. We lived the quintessential American life—a huge house, fancy cars, weekend gateways, and the yearly trips to India. During those trips, I spent most of my vacations on the farm. It was not what it used to be. So, at the back of my mind, I always wanted to nurture it and bring it back to the time of my grandparents."

"As fate would have it, some turn of events brought me back to India initially for extended periods of time and eventually permanently."

"Must have been testing time for you," sympathised Sandhya.

"Yes, you can say that."

"What happened?" asked Sandhya.

"Well, ten years ago my father suffered a stroke. The left side of his body was paralyzed. I reached Pune five days after he was hospitalized. Those five days were traumatic for my mother. It was the first time I felt so helpless. There was nothing I could do for America to ease their pain and suffering. I was to stay for ten days and return. But by the time my father was discharged and in a stable condition to be brought home two weeks had passed. It was difficult for my mother to take charge of the situation. The mere thought of my returning and her having to deal with the situation broke my heart. I managed to convince my boss to grant me leave for a month. He was gracious enough to grant me that leave, despite a heavy workload...also, there was Deepa, it was for the first time she was staying all by herself. She too understood I needed to be here, but it was not easy on her as well."

"It took close to a year for things to settle down. With proper care and appropriate help, my father was on his recovery path. I kept visiting as and when I could."

He continued "During one of my visits I encouraged my parents to visit Satara. All of us realized that my father was happier living at the farmhouse. It took a little longer for my mother to agree but eventually, they started living on the farm. It gave some purpose to their life. As for me, I felt it was the best decision they had taken. This allowed me to be at the farm and look after them whenever I visited."

"My visit in February-March 2020 was the catalyst for my relocation. My return flight was booked for 25th March and lockdown was declared on 22nd. Initially, we thought all of this was temporary. But as days went by it became clear that that lockdown was here to stay for a long time. Thanks to technology I started working from home, but my wife was again forced to be by herself," he reminisced.

"There were four people who lived on the farm besides my parents and myself. They were a great help during that time. It was during that unintended extended stay that I started my experiments with organic farming. Initially, we did face some glitches and setbacks, what with all at sea about growing vegetables organically; a concept totally new to all of us, but within a span of six months we were able to fix the problems and, grow healthy veggies. Soon, we diversified even into grains, and in a corner plot, I even planted some fruit trees. And since then, there has been no looking back. We have been able to grow multiple crops and harvest superior-quality products. Our products are brought by five-star hotels and specialty stores in Pune and Mumbai. My income from the farm exceeded my salary within a couple of months after starting the project. By mid-2022 I quit my job and have been earning handsome money through my organic farming venture. I have permanently shifted back to India and to my passion."

"Don't you miss your life in the US? It must have been so difficult for you to come back permanently," Sandhya asked.

"Honestly, I never felt at home in the US," replied Viraj without hesitation. "For me, it was always a work destination, it was never going to be my permanent home." " When I married Deepa, I had made it known to her too that I was not interested in making the US my permanent home. So, it was not unexpected, only unplanned .... or should I say, earlier than I had planned?"

Sandhya was amazed at the simplicity and openness of Viraj. He shared some important lessons to be learnt especially for the younger generation.

There was just one more question that she had to ask. "Did your wife also want to move back? Was she happy to come back to India too?"

Viraj smiled. He was half expecting this question and was prepared with his answer.

"Look, any decision is tough to make. She was not for it. We had our share of arguments...so we decided to take time off...by that I mean, we decided we will live separately for some time, and see how it work out for both of us ...she would come down for holidays, stay at the farm but was not ready to give up her job. I too did not force her ...after all, it's her life and she have a right to decide how she wants to live it."

He paused. Smiling at her, he said, his eyes twinkling with happiness, said "Deepa after many trips to Satara and seeing my efforts paying off, decided she too would like to come back to her own country. In fact, you would be happy to know that this award ceremony came as a boon for me in that sense too."

On her enquiring look, he continued, "She expedited her plans to wind up her affairs in the US and come earlier than she had planned, just to be there at the function. It was hectic for her as well as for me no doubt, but then, 'all's well that ends well! So, from here we go home to Satara for the first time as a complete family forever."

Sandhya looked at him and felt the happiness emanating from him. She smiled too and was truly happy for him Very few people have the conviction and determination to lead their lives the way they want to, and he was amongst those few. She switched off her Dictaphone and winded up the interview, "It has been great talking to you Viraj, you certainly have walked the untrodden path! Your choices have been uncommon and your journey inspiring."

"I hope the youth who read about you will find inspiration to follow their dreams. All the best to you."

They shook hands and Sandhya walked away, happy with her interview with Viraj and his success story.

Darkest Hour, Brightest Dawn

Col Gaurav Bhatia, PhD (Retd)

When life's tempests rage and all seems lost,
And hope is but a flicker in the dark,
When every earthly prop is overthrown,
And all our strength is but a feeble spark.

It is then that faith reveals its worth,
And trust in God's unchanging love shines bright,
For though the night may be the darkest hour,
The dawn is ever near, a new day's light.

And as the tempest subsides and calm returns,
We find that in our bleakest hour,
God was there, orchestrating all things for our good,
Preparing us for what the future holds,
For when we're bereft of all,
He is up to something transcendent than our hearts can mold.

Heart of Gold

Rita Som

It was a party by the swimming pool. I had reluctantly accompanied my husband, though once there I was drawn to the beautiful ambience created for the evening. I knew very few people. As the party progressed I came across a wonderful Bengali couple who were also new to this place like me. I was drawn towards them. My eyes followed them for some time till we were introduced by the host. Mr. Shamal Gupta had recently joined as the MD of a renowned company. We took an instant liking for each other. The rest of the evening his wife Sagarika and I spent together. Eventually, we became very good friends. In this small, lazy industrial township where I was living since the time I got married, well-organized parties and meeting some wonderful people were the only recreation.

What I instantly liked about this couple was their positive and friendly demeanour. Besides both look so beautiful together made for each other couple. Not only did they glow in their happiness, but they also spread the same all around. I was very happy to meet such a wonderful and lively couple. They started visiting us occasionally in the evenings. We used to laugh, joke, and discuss various topics with a touch of Bengali humour in it.

They had a twenty-year-old son Sujoy, who never accompanied

them. They had a 24/7 helping hand who had come along with them from Kolkata when they shifted here, who would take care of him when they were away. So, no tension.

We once invited them over for dinner and insisted that they should bring along their son too and they obliged. I observed that though in looks he did not match his parents there was something very nice about him. He looked straight into my eyes with a sweet smile all over his face as if to say, 'Look at my inner beauty.' With spectacles on his plump, round face he looked quite mature. He sat quietly next to his mother. Obviously that he was brought to our house with many instructions. He had that sweet smile constantly on his face and he spoke very little.

I knew he was gradually getting connected to me and we started talking. He also came into the kitchen to see what I was serving them. He said he loved chicken with veggies and the dish looked so attractive that he started feeling hungry. I noticed he had some speech problems. He also had coordination problems but with little help from his parents, he ate and enjoyed every preparation. We laughed and talked, and it turned out to be a great evening. We understood that the boy was different. His behaviour too was not age appropriate, but it did not matter at all to me or my husband as he was so well behaved, more than many normal children.

After that day Sujoy always accompanied his parents when they visited us.

Once both our husbands went for a stag party and Sagarika decided to spend the evening with me. The revelations that she made that evening were so touching that my heart was filled with awe and admiration for her. In the end, I just gave her a hug.

She told me that due to some medical problems she could not conceive, so after a lot of contemplation they went for adoption. Before adoption, they attended many awareness programs and counselling too. While they were going through the process and formalities she realised there was a huge waiting period for adopting a normal child but there were many children with developmental disabilities waiting to be adopted.

That kept bothering her and made her think. From all the information that she gathered, she understood that these children face substantial functional limitations in three or more of the following areas of significant life activity—self-care; receptive and expressive language; learning; mobility; capacity for independent living; and economic self-sufficiency. The individual child may need special support and assistance that could be lifelong.

She felt well-equipped and ready for all that. She also understood that children who experience developmental disabilities, like all children, benefit greatly from the stability and love that come from being a part of a permanent family. This ray of hope reaffirmed her decision to adopt a child with special needs. She believed each one of us came here with a purpose. And she thought this could be hers.

Her husband had found her preoccupied and restless for quite some time and one evening asked her as to what was bothering her. She poured her heart out to him. His reaction did not come as a surprise to her. He held her in his arms and whispered in her ears, “Darling I am proud of you. How could you even think that I would not support this noble decision of yours? This is going to be ‘our’ decision.” Without much delay, they went back to complete the adoption formalities and soon they were called to select a child. The smile of a little boy drew them towards him and instantly they knew this would be their child…...

He had a traumatic birth maybe a forceps or suction delivery due to which some nerves and brain cells were damaged. With all the love, care, attention, and support he grew up to be a wonderful man except for a minor lack of physical coordination and the mental age not matching his actual age. She also told me that they were wealthy and had property so much so that three generations could just live on it without doing anything. So, money was not an issue, but her worry was how will he manage in the future when they won't be there.... but that was for later, today was to enjoy his presence and enjoy being parents!

One day they came to meet us and broke the news that they had decided to go back to Kolkata. That made me very sad. They were very upset too but had no choice, they said. They had to think of Sujoy's future. They were particularly sad as they felt ours was the only family that the three of them would be very comfortable with as we never ever questioned them about their son whatsoever and had wholeheartedly accepted him as our own. We bade tearful goodbyes and promised to keep in touch.

Days and months passed. We visited them after some years when we were in Kolkata on a holiday...they welcomed us now along with another lady with a child in her arm. She was their daughter-in-law Rini, and the bubbly little boy was their grandchild. Sujoy along with Rini ran a general store in the heart of the city. He managed the cash counter. Sujoy had great skill in managing accounts and looking after sales besides a knack for maintaining wonderful relations with customers.

I will never ever forget the five faces of this wonderful family with a heart of gold that reflected radiantly on their faces when they bid me goodbye.

The Forbidden Decision

Smriti Agarwal

The following story is based on real life.

The sun was shining bright and Shruti was watering the plants in her garden when she heard the doorbell and wondered who it could be on a Sunday morning.

The caretaker Beena opened the door and after a while, Shruti saw the couple Amit and Ruchika crossing over the beautifully designed living room towards the lawn. She kept the water can on the grass and walked towards the house smiling, "Hey where have you two been? It's been a long time since you last visited us." Ruchika gave her a hug, "We were travelling, just got back yesterday and here we are. We were also dying to meet you both, so we landed here unannounced. Where is Raj?" Shruti made a face and mocked her, "Where is Raj? As if you don't know that he will not wake up before 11 am on a Sunday." Amit laughed, "*Nawabzaada*! (His Highness!) Let me wake him up." He strode towards the staircase leading to the bedroom and swiftly climbed shouting for Raj.

After a few minutes foul language and abuses could be heard from afar, meaning that Amit had woken Raj. Ruchika and Shruti laughed. Shruti told Beena to get the tea and breakfast ready for everyone.

Shruti knew that Amit and Ruchika's second son had also now left for Boston to study further. She asked Ruchika "What news of the boys? How are they?" Ruchika smiled and her face showed that she did miss them. "Both are doing good. Ajay is in his last semester and Tanay will begin his first. It is great when kids do well, and these days parents have to cope with their going away."

Shruti smiled as she was genuinely fond of both the boys. "Yes I remember, how you used to feel the empty nest syndrome, but now look at yourself, enjoying life."

"Look who is talking? You and Raj you never had kids and life has only been a never-ending party for both of you." Before Shruti could react, she saw a disheveled Raj and a smirking Amit coming down the stairs.

Soon they were all chatting and enjoying breakfast on the well-laid dining table. It was customary to have South Indian breakfast on Sundays. Raj was just having his cup of morning tea and said that he would eat later. Amit had given him enough time only to brush his teeth and Raj was in no mood of eating so early.

After Amit and Ruchika left, Shruti made herself comfortable on the garden chair, basking in the early winter sun. Her mind wandered off to the casual remark made by Ruchika. Life was not just a series of parties for them only because they decided not to have children of their own. It was a tough decision and they had to face a lot of flak because of it. It was not easy. At times it got downright tormenting and mentally very stressful.

Shruti and Raj had gotten married fifteen years back, after six years of dating and living, and at the age of thirty-eight when they got married, they had made up their minds that will not reproduce. Well, it was not an easy decision. After all, in India as soon as one gets married, there is an immense amount of societal and family pressure to have kids.

But then, none of their decisions had been easy for them. When they decided to live together, there was an uproar of refusal, drama, and commotion from Shruti's family. Raj's family did not even know that they were deciding something. For them, Shruti was his girlfriend in Delhi while he worked in Chandigarh, but for Shruti to leave Delhi and shift with Raj in Chandigarh was something she had to tell her family. Amidst all the arguments, the argument of an Indian girl to remain a virgin till marriage was the biggest issue. "What if you two break up? Who will marry you then? What are you doing with your life?" were some of the questions her parents threw at her, and she had no answers to such questions. She knew it was pointless. *Arrey*! (Hey) Here even in Bollywood and in a film like *DDLJ* (Dilwale Dulhaniya Le Jayenge, an extremely popular film of the 90s) where both the girl and the boy, born and brought up in London and travelling with friends discovering Europe were supposed to know what is a '*Hindustani ladki ki izzat*' (Indian girl's dignity) even after being drunk and sharing a room in Switzerland (reference here is to a particular scene in the movie). In their case it was even more as the age was catching up and now the 'live in'. Add to that, Shruti's mother's constant lectures on how she had Shruti when she was twenty-four and now Shruti is thirty-four and deciding to live in, not get married, lose her virginity (she did not know that the disaster had already happened), and with her biological clock ticking, when will she finally make babies and live a normal life.

Well, finally the day came when they decided to get married. Both their families were already upset with them for the six long years of dating (for one side) and living together without any commitments (for the other family) and now after finally deciding to marry, they announced their decision not to have kids. Both families went berserk.

Raj was the only son and he had three elder sisters who were happily married and each one had a family to raise. Raj's parents had waited for the longest time for him to find his life partner and ultimately get married to provide them their heir and continue the family lineage. On the day of their wedding Raj's mother told Shruti in Punjabi, *"Bas puttar ab jaldi se ek sona jiya pouta de de tu mainu, tou mai poute da mooh dekh kar chain se apne ankhaa band kar lu."* (Now you have to give me a grandson really quickly so that I can die in peace.) Shruti remained silent and just nodded as there was little she could say as a new bride. On the other side Raj's eldest sister gave him the tickets for the honeymoon and said, "We have booked the trip for you and Shruti to enjoy. Have fun and listen, once you are back, we need some good news real fast." She added, *"Arrey bhai, koi hume bhi tou bua bulane wala ho"* (There should be someone to call us 'aunt.') Raj got irked, and they had a small argument, but his *didi* (elder sister) did not budge. He left it at that for the moment.

Two years had passed after their marriage, and they had not yet given the 'good news' to the family. Speculations began! One day Shruti received a call from her youngest sister-in-law advising her to seek medical help. Shruti, though annoyed, had stifled a laugh. How could she tell them that only last month, she had an abortion? It was not that they could not become parents or that there was an issue conceiving. Shruti often wondered, "Why is it so hard for people to understand and believe that they have consciously decided not to have children?" Raj and Shruti had made up their minds earlier in their relationship not to have kids for various reasons. The main one being they did not believe that another life should be brought into this world to be a part of the ever-growing rat race in the world. They did not agree to give a new life on this earth which was slowly dying. Also, they both were clear that they both would be working and were passionate about their profession and life. There was no space for a child. They never wanted to bring in a life to suffer and that they suffer with her/him for the rest of their lives.

Some people look at it from a pessimistic perspective. Some thought they were absolutely crazy not to do the right thing of having a family. Arguments varied from person to person. "Who will look after you when you are old? How can you not have a child? What's there to look forward to if there are no children?" Some people even suggested that they would get bored of each other and would have nothing to do or live for once they crossed middle age. There were always constant questions, nagging, and advice. Shruti felt bad when the second question for anyone she met was, "So how many kids do you have?" and when she would say, "we have none as we decided not to have kids," sure enough, she would get a gasping stare. Some would not believe her and gossip behind her back that she is actually not a complete woman. Some never trusted that there was no medical issue. Some near and dear ones were so casual and hurting with their unthoughtful comments, Raj and Shruti were never deterred from their stance and were very clear that they would live life as they wanted to and not as society or their family wanted them to. They really enjoyed each other's company and lived life on their own terms. But people never changed. So many of their friends and families never invited them to their children's birthdays thinking, what would they do here? They don't have kids. Raj and Shruti often discussed that socializing or having a good time at the party and meeting friends had nothing to do with not having kids, but the world never saw that perspective.

Slowly, their friends started getting their children married or sending them to different countries for higher studies, and even on all these occasions; they never involved Shruti or Raj. It was equally tough in the office and in the club, where everyone would just discuss their children or the future of their children, and these two could never be a part of any conversation. Why couldn't they suggest a school or university or a career path for the new generation? They were well-educated, travelled, and intelligent people, but the other parents would often sideline their views by saying, "What would do you know, you don't have kids?"

Shruti was still deep in thought when Raj sat in the next chair and called out to Beena in a loud voice. Shruti was startled, and Raj laughed. Shruti hit him with a small cushion. Raj teased her, "Where are you lost, my love?" Shruti shook her head, "Nothing *yaar* (friend)!"

Beena came, and Raj ordered her to get his meal now. Shruti also got up to help Beena with Raj's meal, as he wanted everything placed perfectly. In the kitchen, she told herself for the umpteenth time, "It is our life, and we will lead it as we want and die happy. We are not answerable to anyone."

With a smile, she picked up the brunch tray and called Raj to the dining table.

Bold & Beyond

Vasudha Kapoor Duggal

This is a true story about my mother and her tryst with playing the superwoman in a new terrain and between unknown people. I say new terrain as she has been a homemaker, who moved to Kolkata after marriage from a village in Bihar, who was inhibited and wasn't at all outgoing, and who had never seen a police station or a courtroom except in movies.

Hailing from Kolkata, we moved to Delhi in 1984. This story is from 1992, just a couple of years after I got married. I had left some of my jewellery in my mom's house as I didn't have a bank locker of my own. My mom intended to put it all in her locker on the following Saturday. Since Saturday was a good five days away, she had to keep the jewellery safe till then. So, she put them in 3-4 pouches and slid them far deep under her Godrej almirah. Yes, UNDER the almirah. This bright idea, she says she got from the film *Angoor* (A Hindi Film) when actor Deven Verma does the same, expecting any thief to look inside the almirah but not under it!!

But on the third day, on checking, my mom found those pouches missing! She was alarmed and absolutely devastated! Especially since most of it was my wedding jewellery. She frantically searched her almirah, having self-doubts about where she had put them. When my father returned from work, she checked with him, and only when he had confirmed that she had hidden the pouches under the almirah did her search stop.

The next day, Mom was in no mood to do her daily house chores and waited for Mamta, her cleaning maid, to arrive. But Mamta didn't turn up. That roused her suspicion. The following day, again, she didn't turn up. When the maid didn't show up for three-four days, it confirmed my mom's suspicion. Thereafter one day, while buying lemons from a cart vendor passing the house, she asked him if he knew her maid or her whereabouts. Luckily, he did know her as she was from the same village and informed my mother that she had been sitting at home for a few days and had earlier told him she intended to go to her village in Bengal and buy a new fishing net. The next day after checking at her place, Naresh, the cart vendor, informed Mom that Mamta had already left for her village.

A week passed in extreme anguish. My father insisted on reporting this at the local police station, though everyone felt that little could be expected from the police unless some big amount was doled out. Since my father was strictly against any kind of bribery, this option was never even considered. Nonetheless, the complaint was lodged. But something had to be done. They couldn't just depend on the police. Mom was very clear she wasn't going to let the maid get away with the jewellery. Then, after much discussion at home and with my *masi* (mother's sister) in Varanasi, my mother decided to take some concrete action by taking matters into her own hands.

She decided to go to the maid's village and nab her. We tried to deter her, as times were not good, and it could be risky. But my mother's mind was made up. Since my *mausa ji* (mother's brother-in-law) had agreed to accompany her, we relented. She spoke to Naresh, the vegetable vendor, who was more than willing to help and who also offered to reach the village. So, Mom left for Varanasi, where her sister stayed. From there, after a day's rest, she departed for Farakka in Bengal by train with Anandji, her brother-in-law. Naresh had already reached Farakka on the designated date and met up with them at the Farakka railway station early in the morning.

Farakka is a very small town in Murshidabad district of Bengal. However, Mamta lived in a village in the interiors where Naresh was to take them. The journey happened on a bullock cart and took about three hours.

It was quite a rocky ride as the roads were mostly unmetalled *kuchha* (uncemented) roads. Towards the end of the journey, they had to take a boat to cross a large *talaab* (water body). Getting into the wobbly boat wasn't as easy as it looked. My mom was tense, and the boatman's chatter about the countryside did little to alleviate her mood. The water was still and very clean, and it took another thirty minutes to cross it. After alighting from the boat, they had to walk some distance, with Naresh leading the way, until they reached the house belonging to the maid, Mamta.

They encountered Mamta right outside her house, where she was busy drying clothes. She was shell-shocked on seeing my mother there. My mother spoke to her gently; asked her how she was and why she suddenly came to the village. Mamta muttered something inaudible. Then Mom quietly told her that she knew she had taken her jewellery and urged her to return it so she would then close the issue and return to Delhi, failing which she would have to complain to the police. Mamta denied taking it but retorted that how come, my mom, thought of her jewellery after almost a month! This further confirmed all doubts. Mom was hoping Mamta would admit to her felony and hand her all the jewellery to avoid the police. But as my *mausaji* told her, it was wishful thinking.

After Mamta continued to deny it, Naresh told her that they would go to the police and the consequences wouldn't be good. As my mom, *mausaji*, and Naresh returned, some other local villagers standing around, enquired after them and requested them to come inside their hut and offered water. Thirsty as they were, they entered one of the huts, and Mom recalls how spic and span the hut was. The villager quickly spread out a clean white sheet on the *charpai* (rope bed) and asked them to sit before offering water in *kulhars* (earthen cups). He told them that Mamta had earlier also stolen some goods and got away in the absence of any police complaint. He encouraged them to report to the *thana* (local police station).

Thereafter, commenced the return journey starting with the boat ride. It was three pm when, led by Naresh, the vegetable vendor, they reached the local police station. A lot of time elapsed in lodging a formal complaint there. The fact that Mom could speak Bengali really helped. Contrary to the negative impression everyone had about the police, they were extremely polite and helpful. Once the FIR (First Information Report) was lodged, the police immediately deputed two-three police personnel to go to Mamta's place. However, by the time the police reached her place, she had absconded. When they returned, Naresh then told them of the possibility of her having run to her mother's place in Jangipur and provided the whereabouts. The search team then mounted their scooters and left for Jangipur.

Meanwhile, my mom and *mausaji* were waiting at the police station, hungry and tired. The police were kind enough to offer them tea and biscuits.

Late in the evening, the search team returned with the stolen stuff. They informed that Mamta had hidden the pouches in a box that was inside four cases of increasing sizes, the biggest being a suitcase-sized aluminium box! As soon as they said they had got the stuff, my mom's relief and joy knew no bounds. She profusely thanked them all, including Naresh, without whose assistance this could have been a very uphill task. But before opening the pouches, the police asked my mother to list the stolen items. Her list matched the items inside. The police convinced that my mother was the rightful owner, apprised her that now the due process of law will have to be followed, and the items would first have to be deposited in Court. Unfortunately, the Court formality got delayed by three days, as two days the judge was on leave, and on the third day, the court was closed due to some holiday.

Meanwhile, that very evening, my mother and *Mausaji* needed a place to put up for the night. They both recall how nice and cooperative the police had been, unlike all their initial misgivings. The local police also helped find accommodation for them by requesting one Mr. Jain, an affluent local businessman, who had a huge *Kothi* (house), to provide them lodging. Mr Jain and his family very graciously hosted my mother and *Mausaji* for two days. The Jain ladies played the perfect host as they served delicious food to their guests during their stay. To date, my mom fondly recalls some of the dishes she had eaten there.

And while so much drama happened in Farakka, we in Delhi were anxious about them and kept hoping for their success and quick return. For the next three days, my mom and *mausaji* passed their time walking down the countryside, playing cards, and generally chit-chatting with the Jain family.

After three long days, the court formalities started. Mom was asked to narrate her story and record her statement. Surprisingly, she did not have to stand in the witness box like the rest, as the judge, on his own, allowed her to speak from where she was sitting, as she was a *bhadra mahila* (gentle/decent lady). Mamta, the maid, was interrogated. She confessed to her crime and was immediately put behind bars. My mom was asked to submit a bond of Rs. 5000/- and bills and receipts of the recovered jewellery. Since she wasn't carrying any bills, she declared that she would return in a few days with all the papers. For the first time in her life, my mother had entered a court and a police station where she saw criminals being beaten, some crying and wailing, and relatives pleading amidst all the commotion.

The next morning, with this initial formality completed, they started their return journey, first to the station. This time they took an open tempo to the station in which there were three-four other men already sitting. During that half-hour drive, Mom heard these men talk amongst themselves about a *bhadra mahila* who had come from Delhi and how she had recovered her jewellery, completely unaware that that *bhadra mahila* was travelling with them. They were referring to a local Bengali newspaper, which carried an article about my mom and her jewellery recovery story. Comprehending all that they were speaking in Bengali, my mom smiled happily as she translated the conversation to Anandji, her brother-in-law.

And while Mom was on this recovery mission in Bengal, we at home went through a harrowing time. Those days there weren't any cell phones. So, once she left Varanasi, we had lost touch with her. There was no news of her. We did not know where she was, how she was, and whether she was safe. The only small consolation was that her brother-in-law was with her, and she was not alone. Yet, all kinds of scary thoughts crossed our minds. We couldn't sleep, and some of my other relatives, who were also panicking, kept calling me as we voiced our fears together. All of us started praying for their safe return.

Once Mom was back in Delhi, all required bills and receipts were quickly searched and collected. A week later, my dad took leave from his office to accompany her to Farakka. My dad's brother-in-law Mr Sarin, who is a lawyer, also accompanied them. Unlike the earlier tense train journey, this journey was an enjoyable one, as my parents and uncle played cards, chatted, and joked like their usual times.

Once in Farakka, the documents were submitted in Court, and all formalities were completed. The stolen jewellery was handed over to my mother. Everything was intact except one *kara* (bangle) which was broken into three-four pieces and one piece was missing. The maid had sold that small piece and probably bought herself a new fishing net. My mother, of course, was on cloud nine.

Once back home, there was a barrage of congratulatory and complimentary messages for my mom. She too felt as if she had a major accomplishment to her credit. For days all we did was talk about her adventure to all and sundry. And yes, how my mom enjoyed narrating everything to all who asked her. Normally after a theft, people lodged their police complaint and then at best, followed up with the police. Here, Mom decided to take things into her own hands and dared to go to Mamta's village and encounter her. It was a risky proposition in an unknown area. Luckily, everyone whom she encountered in her quest turned out to be very decent and cooperative, starting from Naresh, the cart vendor. With the mission successful, Mom was a sight to behold as everyone talked of her courage and determination to recover her stuff. And she had a hearty laugh when a relative remarked, *"Ratna Kapoor hamari Jhansi ki Rani hai"* (Our Ratna Kapoor is Queen of Jhansi).

Miracles and Magic

Praneel Dev

Life is full of miracles and magic.
Sparks of wonder burn through tragic.
Suspenseful surprises make it dramatic.
Out with boredom, end of static.

Life is full of poise and purpose.
Opportunities galore with chances surplus
Attractions enough to run a circus.
Wanting, prancing for our focus.

Life is full of humour and hope.
Sunlit beach walks are my favourite trope.
Or with thundering evenings, problems? nope
Of distress and despair, cut their rope.

Life is full of celebration and cheer.
The song of laughter is soulful to hear.
You only live once, so cherish it, dear.
Happy hearts have nothing to fear.

Bhairavi—The Brave

Zeyd Ladha

Disclaimer: *The following story is a fictionalised account of Mewar Kingdom, of Rajasthan in India. The characters and the incidents narrated are a figment of the writer's imagination. They bear no resemblance to the authentic part of Mewari history.*

The soldiers opened the gates to the palace of Mewar. Hundreds of horsemen, who were holding up the kingdom's outer defence, waited outside. A few entered the palace complex.

"We wish to meet the king," requested Madhav, the general.

The doors to the palace were opened, and they were allowed to meet the king.

"What news do you bring, Madhav?" asked Maharaj Ratan Singh.

"I'm afraid the news is not good, Maharaj."

"Speak now; what is it?"

"Our outer defence has been breached and...." he stopped.

"And what, Madhav?"

Madhav could not muster the courage to speak. Maharaj looked around and realised his son was missing.

"Where is my son Madhav? Tell me now!" shouted Maharaj.

"I'm sorry, Maharaj, he fell trying to keep the enemy at bay."

"What do you mean he fell?"

Madhav moved aside, and four soldiers carried a casket to the king. They placed it down and moved the cloth from the face of the body.

Maharaj Ratan Singh was shattered from within but had to maintain his composure. The queen, Beena, though, couldn't hold back her tears. She ran to her son, put her head on his chest, and wept profusely.

"How did this happen, Madhav?"

"He fought like a tiger," said Madhav. "Five enemy soldiers couldn't bring him down, then two more came, and then two more. Nine were too many even for a mighty warrior like him."

"My son is a martyr; he died defending his kingdom. His sacrifice will not go in vain. What is our status, Madhav?"

"Not good, Maharaj," replied Madhav. "Ten thousand strong soldiers march upon us. We are outnumbered."

Maharaj Ratan Singh walked back to this throne and sat down. He thought for some time.

"Beena, you must take Princess Bhairavi, the women, and the children to safety through the secret passage that leads into the woods. From there you will have to go to Jaipur. The Maharaja of Jaipur will give you shelter and protection. Madhav, gather our full force. We will defend our gate at any cost."

"But father," protested Bhairavi, "I can fight! So can the other young women. Let us fight beside you."

"No, my daughter," said Maharaj. "I have already lost a son today; I cannot lose my daughter too."

"I grieve for my brother too," said Bhairavi, staring sternly at her brother. "I wish to fight in his stead. I wish to avenge him."

"That is enough," Maharaj thundered. "You will obey me like how other women obey me. You will go out through the secret passage. That is an order!"

"How much time do we have, Madhav, before the enemy is at our gate?"

"Two days, Maharaj."

"Bhairavi, you must gather the women and children and leave tonight," instructed Maharaj.

"Yes, Father," she agreed and left the palace.

"Madhav, assemble your army tonight. At the break of dawn, we leave for battle."

"Why do we ride out so soon?" enquired Madhav.

"I want to meet the enemy in battle as far away as possible from my home, my kingdom," explained Maharaj. "Let's get moving; we have no time to waste."

Madhav bowed and hurried out.

Maharaj Ratan Singh noticed his wife had been quiet. Once the others had left, he walked up to her.

"Are you okay, my love?"

She quickly wiped her tears. "We have no time to grieve for our son. I am worried for you and our people. Why is this happening to us?"

"We have enjoyed our days of abundance, my queen. We never asked then, why us? This is a difficult time, but you must have faith; this too shall pass."

"How can I not be worried? You ride out to battle, where your army will be heavily outnumbered! What if?" she couldn't speak any further.

"If the worst should happen, look after Bhairavi. She is hot-headed. She will seek revenge, but you must ask her to take her time. Build an army, rebuild your strength, and then attempt to retake what rightfully belongs to her."

"You know her very well," said Beena. "It will be difficult to hold her back. But I promise you I will try."

At dusk, the army had assembled at the gate of Mewar Palace. Bhairavi had managed to get the women and children in as well. Maharaj Ratan Singh walked out of his palace, wearing his full armour, his sheathed sword on his waist, and his helmet in one hand. He stood outside the main door before alighting the stairs.

"My men, listen to me," he started his speech. "These are dark times indeed, but it is only in darkness that a *diya* can show its brilliant flame. Such times come to test our mettle. We are Rajput warriors! We have never given up without a fight, and we never will. We ride out now to war and maybe to death, but if this is to be our end, we will make it worthy of remembrance. We will make the enemy repent the day they decide to attack us, the Rajput tigers. I am honoured today to fight beside each one of you. I pray to our mighty Goddess to bless us and make us victorious."

"And I pray for you to return victorious," said Beena. She brought a *pooja thali* (plate decorated with items of worship) for prayer and performed a prayer for her husband. She applied a red saffron mark on his forehead and said, "May *Mata* (Goddess) bless you with victory."

"Jai Mata Di!" (Glory to the Goddess) shouted the king.

"Jai Mata Di," said all the soldiers in unison.

Maharaj climbed down the stairs of his palace and mounted his horse. He rode out of the palace, followed by Madhav and his army.

Once the army had left and the palace gate secured, Beena guided the women and children to the secret passage. Bhairavi helped her to get everyone out. Once all the women and children had left, the soldiers who stayed back sealed the passage and barricaded the entrance. It was dark inside the passage; the flame of their torch was all that was lighting up their way. A few minutes later, they arrived at a fork.

"Mother, you must take the others and go right. That way leads to the forest and to Jaipur palace," said Bhairavi.

"What about you?" asked Beena.

"I will take the passage left," said Bhairavi. "It leads into *Mukundara forest*, home of *Aadhiren* (Jungle King) and the forest people."

Beena was shocked. "Why? Why, dear Bhairavi? The forest people are dangerous, merciless killers. None who ventured into that forest have ever returned."

"I know they are dangerous, Mother, which is why I am going there. I will ask them to fight for us!"

"They fight only for themselves; they answer to no one."

"I believe I can convince them. I must do this, Mother, please. It is the only hope for Father and our army."

Reluctantly Beena agreed. "Go then, my daughter. May Mata bless you with success in what you seek."

"Thank you, Mother," said Bhairavi and broke away from the group.

At the end of the passage, a beautiful white mare awaited her. She mounted her mare and rode confidently into a forest most men feared to step foot into. She rode straight to *Aadhiren's* abode.

"You are a brave young woman to enter my forest," said *Aadhiren* in his baritone voice.

"I come to seek the help of the mighty forest people."

"I have heard of the war that is upon Mewar. But it is not our battle. Why should we fight for you anyways? Your father has never recognised us; he and his men do not allow us to dwell peacefully in the forest. They think of us as troublemakers and enemies of the state. Let him fall; why should we care?"

"You have to fight for us, you belong to these lands and these lands belong to you. You will have to help me defend our lands. You know the enemy will come after you next, don't you?"

"No one dares step foot into my forest. You have dared to do that, and I can have your head for that!"

Bhairavi drew her sword, looked straight into *Aadhiren's* eyes, and said, "Try it!"

The men burst into laughter.

"As feisty as her father," said *Aadhiren*. "I admire your grit and courage; we will fight for you, young princess. But we have our terms. After the victory, we want control of these forests. We are to be left to ourselves."

"And you will not kill anyone from our kingdom."

"I think we have a deal then!" exclaimed *Aadhiren*.

On the battlefront, Maharaj Ratan Singh, Madhav, and his army stood poised for attack. The strength of the enemy in numbers was much greater than the Mewar army.

"We are heavily outnumbered, Maharaj," said Madhav.

"I know Madhav, but they have no idea about the courage and strength of the Rajputs."

Suddenly, a rider appeared over the adjoining hill. The rider carried the flag of Mewar.

"Maharaj, who is that?" asked Madhav, pointing to the mysterious rider.

Maharaj looked closely, and the long hair of the rider gave away her identity. "Bhairavi!"

Then another rider appeared. It was *Aadhiren*. *Aadhiren* was a big man with long hair and a big beard. He looked menacing even from a distance. Then more riders appeared on the mountain top.

"*Aadhiren* and his forest people!" exclaimed Maharaj.

"Can the forest people be trusted?" asked Madhav.

"My daughter rides with him, Madhav. Surely, we can trust them."

"To the king!" she instructed as she and *Aadhiren* and his men rode down the mountain slope to fight beside the king. The forest people formed a line behind the Mewar army. Bhairavi and *Aadhiren* took their position at the front beside the king and Madhav. The tables had turned; the enemy was now scared. *Aadhiren* and the forest people were notorious as ferocious fighters and merciless murderers.

"I'm proud to fight beside you, Bhairavi. Let's take them down," said Maharaj confidently. "Sound the charge!"

An epic battle raged, which ended in a thumping victory for Mewar. A battle that could have seen the end of Mewar now established it as one of the most powerful kingdoms of Bharat. History altered its course when one courageous young girl decided to take the untrodden path!

Befriending Struggle

Asad Chaugule

A thirst for triumph,
Has aurified my onerous path,
Despite loving the canorous voice of winning,
I have aided myself in struggling.

Being denigrated by the defeats in the past,
Deluged by the losses, having surpassed.
Has patronized me to tussle,
Has increased my fondness for hustle.

Let the sunrise for others be premature.
Let their goals be diaphanous,
Being intimated by grinding for sure,
A vivacious achievement will just be a bonus.

Destinations were never promised,
Success was never assured,
From the chisel of hardships,
A statue of victory is carved.

Breaking the Barrier

Neelam Singh

A medical camp was set up in Patna to help the needy women. Dr. Shashi Mishra was invited with other doctors from Mumbai to attend the camp, considering the dearth of doctors there. Though not very inclined to go there but being her home state, she finally decided to go to their aid.

She was examining a sixteen-year-old malnourished girl who was pregnant for the second time. She was accompanied by her mother-in-law. When she asked for details, she was told that the girl had been married off at thirteen, had her first child—a girl—at the age of fifteen, and now she was pregnant again, and it was in the dire interest of her family that she gave birth to a boy. The fact that she was pregnant within such a short time seemed not to be worrying them; the fact that she was so obviously malnourished and weak was of least interest to them; they only wanted that she delivered a 'boy'. There was a big crowd of similar women waiting for medical advice.

*****

The morning events sent Dr Shashi down memory lane into her past, around some fifty years back. She was born in Mumbai to Bihari Brahmin parents as their first child. Her father was in the Railways, and she was admitted to a convent school like all the other children around her. A bright girl, she always outshone others and did well in both academics and extra-curricular activities, but irrespective of that, till she reached the seventh grade, she was sent to their native village at any time of the year on the whims and fancy of her parents.

When she turned fourteen, she was abruptly removed from the school and sent back to the village. She noticed drastic changes in parents' and other family members—hush whispers and quiet group discussions. She was left to wonder about the spurt of activity around her, and she kept mulling about it without having any clue about what was to happen. A deep sense of foreboding slowly enveloped her, nonetheless. Sure enough, soon, her fears were confirmed when she was married off at the tender age of fourteen. The social pressures got the better of her quite an intelligent father who had come out of Bihar to secure a good future for himself and his family.

Mercifully, some sense had prevailed in her parents, and they got her back with them to continue with her studies. Nonetheless, it was embarrassing for her to be the only married girl in the class, though to overcome that, she concentrated on her studies and did brilliantly after that.

The girls in Bihar were not allowed access to higher education back then, but now she was motivated and had a strong desire to become a highly educated and independent person—both emotionally and financially. Luckily for her, her parents though still divided between two thought processes, supported her decision to study further but were pressured to perform her "Guana." *(Guana is an age-old and antiquated practice in Bihar and some states of India, where the girls married off before puberty are sent off to their marital homes with lots of pomp and show after they start menstruating).* This vile act of making public a woman's menstrual cycle and mass celebrating the fact abhorred her since she had first heard it. And now, she was being pressured to go through it.

But to her immense surprise and happiness, her father resisted the enormous and backbreaking societal pressure and supported his daughter to pursue her dreams at the risk of being "OUTCAST" from society, a huge social fear in their community. For that, she is and will remain eternally grateful to her father, for giving her a chance of leading an educated and fulfilled life.

She grew from school to medical college with a determination to change something for the women down there. This time her father was in full support, notwithstanding the norms that have been set. She, as usual, was doing very well and was admitted to the reputed Grant Medical College when came another twist. She fell in love with a Sikh boy an aspiring doctor, leading to another big turmoil in her family and around. This time she was adamant about following her heart, and her dad realised this went with her wishes, however much duress and turmoil that may cause in their community. She completed her medical degree (MBBS) with flying colours and bagged the first rank in Gynaecology in her class. She has now been admitted doing MD. She wanted to be a gynaecologist and help underprivileged women in society.

Now the task at hand was to work to annul the child marriage.

As was expected, the boys' parents did not agree, as this was a huge insult to them, and what would the *baradari* (society) say? But this time, her father stood firm and maybe wanted to make up for all the distress he had caused her in her childhood. Who knows, by now, he had also realised the grave mistake he had made by coming under society's pressure—the useless and backward tradition of child marriage. Rising against all these odds and knowing that the boy is a gem and will keep his daughter happy, he becomes determined to help her to follow her dream. The child marriage was finally behind them, thanks to her father's support and determination.

To her immense happiness, she was married to the person of her choice, and the wedding was performed in a Gurudwara as per the Sikh rituals. She continued with her education.

Giving birth to her first daughter, following a career abroad, followed by the birth of a second daughter born abroad, fully supported by her husband to go in for a successful career, she slowly treads the path of success and almost forgets the turmoil of childhood. Unfortunately, though, the society she was born in never let them forget this, and once, during her father's visit to Patna, his hometown, he faced a life-threatening attack at the railway station. That effectively put an end to all the visits to his home state!

*****

Jerked to the present by being prodded gently by the nurse, she looked at the women, rather girls, who had been thrown into the same predicament from which she had escaped years back. She thanked God for her sheer will power and resilience, which made it possible for her to walk on the untrodden path till then and vowed to make society aware of the dangers of child marriage and early pregnancies. Briskly examining the patient in front of her, she admonished her mother-in-law for pushing the young girl into another unwanted pregnancy and warned her that she will act against her and her son if it happened too soon again. She also threatened to go to the authorities if they harmed their daughter-in-law, in case she delivered a girl child again. This was her usual norm whenever she came to small villages in the interiors of the country with the medical camps.

It made her ponder on the co-existing two diverse worlds, one which is modern and educated and the other still living in the past. She felt blessed to be able to serve the cause of underprivileged women and was thankful that she, in her small measure, was helping them to break the shackles of powerful societal bonds.

A Dream

Augusta Vimla Vincent

Each one's life is a path created by destiny,
Each one has a path of his own.
The untrodden path which no one else experienced.

A path of fame and glory for some,
A path of crime and wickedness for some others,
A path of happiness and peace for a few.

Each one's upbringing decides his path.
The family has a role to play.
The parents are the role model for children.

But it may not be true always.
For pious parents may have wicked children.
The circumstances, too, play a major role.

Whatever it be, each one has an untrodden story to tell!
That's life. No two individuals are alike.
That's the work of the creator.

No two individuals have a similar untrodden path.
Life is unique for each one...
Try to choose the path of righteousness.

Let there be an era of peace among individuals,
Among nations, among leaders, and among citizens...
Let an era of peace and joy reign in this world.

Let each one brings a change that lasts forever and ever...
Let it not be a dream unfulfilled.
Let my dream come true!

Maybe in the near future,
A world of peace and no wars...
Only peaceful discussions and common decisions

Will my dream come true?

Will I be able to see such a world?

A world where peace and harmony reign as the supreme power!

Let all untrodden paths lead to my dream.

Let it be everyone's dream...

Let it be everyone's dream...

Durga Pratima

Aditi Lahiry

"No one is going to buy this idol of yours. Why don't you stop making these idols? Don't you know that it's not a women's job? Who is going to buy this? Have you not seen the idols made by Ramesh Pal or Raghav Das? Everyone rushes to buy their idols only. They have been creating the best idols over the last three-decade or so. The best pandals of the city are flooded with their masterpieces."

Uma was shocked to hear the words of her *pishima* (paternal aunt). Born in a family of potters, she was the only woman who had dared to show her interest in making *Durga Pratimas* (idols of Durga). As a child, she used to watch her father making idols for hours. She still remembered the day when she created her first *Ekchala Pratima* (All the idols were made to fit under a single frame.) just while playing with her friends when she was studying in grade eight. It turned out to be a really good one. She enjoyed taking challenges. She was never afraid to take risks.

"Uma, eta tui baniyechish Ma?" (Is this made by you, Uma?) Ashith had asked her, feeling amazed at his daughter's creation. He encouraged her to make small idols of Laxmi, Kartik, and Saraswati from the next year itself.

Ashith had very high hope for his sons Rudra and Palash. He

used to spend hours teaching them the basics of making the idols after collecting clay, hay, wires, paints, and other raw materials to construct the basic structure called the '*kathamo*'. Palash took a great interest in learning the skill, but for some reason, her father would never allow Uma to learn the skills to make the bigger idols.

She requested Palash that year after a group of young girls from the distant town of Rampur approached them.

"We are organizing an All Women's Sarbojonin Durga Puja in our township. We would appreciate it if the idol were made by Uma," the secretary of The Women's Association of Rampur Cement township, Geeta, said.

"Our organization gives new openings to girls and women potters and artists, especially to those who are trying to set their foot and establish themselves for the first time. Will you be able to make the *Durga Pratima* Uma?"

Throughout the day, Uma tried her best to build up her courage to ask Palash if she could lay her hands on this project. Aashith paralyzed a year ago, just before *Mahalaya*. Rudra and Palash had tried their best levels to complete the ten sets of *Durga Pratima*. Unfortunately, they could not complete it. Uma had saved the situation at that time.

"Palash Da aar Rudra Da, aamae ektibar sujog dao aami aei pratima gulo korte chai" (Oh, Palash Da and Rudra Da, give me one chance to complete these idols).

Thus, because of her request Palash and Rudra agreed to take her help too, and with great difficulty, they managed to complete the idols by *Panchami*.

Rudra and Palash were amazed at the way Uma had really helped them. Her skillful hands worked efficiently, especially while carving the eyes, lips, ears, and nose. She gained a lot of confidence. This year too, she did not want to lose the golden opportunity. She tried to convince her brothers that she wanted to complete this whole project all by herself and her team of girls.

"Yes, you are good at making the idols; we are really impressed by your talent. We want you to help us with our dream project. We are there to support you. Don't worry about Pishima. She will soon realise that what you will create will be a masterpiece," Uma's brothers told her.

Pishima was standing near the main gate of Aashith Pal's studio when Geeta arrived with the cheque and asked the girls of her township to place the *Ekchala Durga Pratima* inside the tempo. Pishima watched the entire scene, feeling astonished.

"The times have indeed changed. Uma has indeed shown me that nothing is impossible if we are determined. *Durga Pratima* can be made by Uma. The girls with her are equally capable and talented."

Uma entered Aashith's room and cried out, holding his hands.

"Baba aami perechi Durga Pratima banate. (Father, I was able to make the idol of Durga.)

Aashith tried to bless his daughter. Tears rolled down his cheeks that day. Uma knew that her father was proud of her. She had taken the risk to walk on the untrodden path, and she was able to ultimately create a niche for herself.

King-Con

Vivek Gulati

Peering through the small gaps in the window of the police van, Mahesh Pratap Singh looked at the sea of faces surrounding him. Swarmed by an army of policemen, one would expect his face to be shadowed with fear and guilt. Instead, he smiled. The once-celebrated IPS Officer smiled as he remembered how the same hands that cuffed him and pushed him through the courtroom today used to salute him not very long ago. Oh, how times have changed!

His crime? He was sentenced to life imprisonment for murdering the Chief Minister.

But why? Why would a sincere, hardworking IPS officer kill the chief of state? The one he's sworn to protect? For answers, we must start at the beginning.

Mahesh was an honest and would-be-a-star IPS officer stationed in a highly volatile border state of India. He had a brilliant academic record and excelled in games like basketball and volleyball at the state level. Standing at six feet plus a few odd inches, he was strongly built and was a black belt in judo. No wonder he was the topper at the Police Training Institute in Hyderabad. All his female batch mates used to have a crush on him and eyed him as perfect boyfriend material.

He was awarded the President's gold medal for gallantry early in his career. He led a team entrusted to eliminate dreaded terrorists who had infiltrated the state from the neighbouring country. Under Mahesh's watchful guidance, the team created a record by eliminating eight terrorists without suffering any casualties. He was the leader any team member would wish for.

Mahesh's childhood wasn't as comfortable as most. His father was a head clerk in a government department that was known for making money. He had resisted all allurement and played by the rule book, much to the anger of his office colleagues and the businessmen who deviously wanted work tenders in their favour. When denied what they wanted, they all ganged up against Mahesh's father, framed him, and got him suspended in a false case of corruption. Not to be disheartened, his father took up giving tuition and preparing his students for examinations.

Despite their struggles, Mahesh's parents gave him one thing in abundance—strong values. They taught him never to throw away his morals, no matter the pressure or the allure of a swanky life.

The apple didn't fall far from the tree. True to his father's values, Mahesh practised all that his parents had taught him. He was known for his forth righteousness and being straightforward in his dealings, to the extent of being blunt. He withstood allurements from businessmen and pressure from seniors and politicians alike. At the end of the day, serving the public and the country was what he wanted to do, and he did it truthfully. He did what he felt was right for the welfare of the public and played by the book.

He didn't see a rank; all he saw was the truth. So much so that the Chief Minister (CM) got angry with him for arresting his close associates who were peddling drugs from across the border, deprived from his main source of income; the CM was livid. He asked his office to convey his displeasure to the DGP and got Mahesh transferred to an insignificant post in Police Administration as a punishment.

Mahesh had no choice but to oblige, but he grew more and more restless over time. Stripped of being able to help the public, he grew frustrated that he was unable to make a difference. One day Mahesh received a call from a renowned social activist—Nageshwar Babu. He had run many campaigns against corruption and was becoming a pain for the current CM. He was instrumental in exposing the CM and his associates; in fact, he was the one who gave Mahesh the tip of drug peddling from across the border, which led to the arrest of the CM's associates.

His voice was trembling, and he could barely get out a word. Mahesh tried to calm him, and that's when he told him that he was getting threats from CM's men. He was being threatened, by mysterious calls telling him they would 'eliminate' him if he doesn't stop campaigning against the CM.

Mahesh was shocked, but a victim of his position and told him clearly, "Sir, you understand I am side-lined in the system. I don't think I will be of much help to you."

Nageshwar Babu insisted, "Beta, you can come out of the system and help me fight corruption." Mahesh was taken aback. No matter the circumstances, he was proud of his job. Leaving his pride behind was something he hadn't ever dreamt of. Gathering some courage, he said, "*Babuji* (father), for us middle-class people, a job is the only source of sustenance. How will I survive without my job?"

Nageshwar Babu just smiled and said, "You are fighting for the right cause, and with courage and patience, everything will follow." Mahesh was taken aback but asked *Babuji* to give him some time to think. It wasn't that Mahesh disagreed, but he was struggling with what to do. Which path was the right one?

Mahesh went to his village and spoke with his father. He was surprised to learn that his father was an active member of *Babuji's* Sangharsh Samiti and was doing extensive work with his organization. He was getting the people of his area together to join *Babuji's* fight against corruption and the current government. His father immediately told him, "Beta, people like *Babuji* come once in a lifetime on this planet and fight for a cause that only uplifts mankind. Just follow him blindly, and only good will happen to you." Hearing reassuring words from his father, all his worries dissipated. Satisfied, he immediately called *Babuji* and told him, "Babuji, it will be my honour to join your movement, and I hope that some of your goodness will rub off on me in the process."

Mahesh's resignation became huge news, and naturally, the bold move created a lot of buzz. As a result, *Babuji's* movement got a big impetus with Mahesh's joining *'Bhrashtrachaar Virodhi Andolan'* (Fight against corruption). CM's men went into overdrive and, desperate, started digging dirt on Mahesh and his family. And then the news started making rounds that Mahesh's father was suspended on charges of corruption. But the public perception of *Babuji* and Mahesh's persona was so strong that all connivers failed. The more negativity was thrown from the CM's PR machinery, the stronger the anti-corruption and anti-CM movement became.

Immediately after joining the movement, Mahesh started strengthening the security around *Babuji*. He got the best and most reliable from those who had previously worked with him. *Babuji* was flushed with public donations, and all his men and Mahesh were well compensated. Mahesh used to give intelligence inputs against drug peddlers and terrorists to his peers still in the police force, and the crime network of the state was severely dented.

Their movement's success snowballed, and the CM was feeling the pressure as the anti-corruption campaign led by *Babuji* was eroding his popularity. Thanks to Mahesh, most of the CM's men were behind bars, and funds were depleting quicker than he could count.

The rising popularity of *Babuji* brought the CM in trouble in more ways than one. With the rapid advancement of the movement, all the cabinet ministers resigned from their posts and joined *Babuji's* movement. Chaos reigned, and the Governor had to take over. The state was in a constitutional flux, and the Governor ordered fresh elections to be held in the state in six months.

Mahesh and his father were elated at the victory of *Babuji's* movement and took pride in playing an important role in shutting out the corrupt CM. One day, Mahesh was walking in the park near his house when he received a call from his father. Unable to conceal his excitement, in a trembling voice, he said, "Beta do you know that *Babuji* is in the running for the next elections? With the support from all the ministers of the ex-CM, I'm sure he will win too."

Mahesh didn't know how to process such huge news. He had no inkling that *Babuji* had any political aspirations, even though he had been closely associated with him for quite some time now. He wondered how he could have missed such important information, given he had such a significant role to play in making his movement a success.

With a million questions racing through his head, he couldn't sit still. With an unsettled mind, he went to meet *Babuji*, and as soon as he saw him, *Babuji* immediately left his posse of ex-ministers and hugged him. *"Aao beta, mere shoorveer, asli taj to tumhare sir par rakhna chahiye."* (Come my son, my warrior, it is you who deserves to be felicitated)

Mahesh touched *Babuji's* feet and pulled him aside, whispering, "Can I talk to you privately?" *Babuji* led him to his office and beamed at him. "Yes, my son, tell me what's bothering you," *Babuji* asked Mahesh. "Babuji, I can't question your decision, but I am eager to know, what prompted you to join politics. When did you decide? *Babuji* let out a small smile. "I was expecting this question from you. Honestly? All my followers from around the state have pressurized me to join politics as they feel that I can make a real difference in shunting out corruption by being inside the system. The head of the table they can trust."

He added, "In fact, I was going to call you today. I want you to be by my side and join me, as unless we have good people in the system, we have no right to criticize. So, will you stand by me?"

Mahesh was speechless. This was the furthest thing from what he had expected. After a few moments, he regained composure and replied, "No, *Babuji*, I would like to be excused. However, I promise my unwavering support as before."

Shortly after, Mahesh joined an NGO and started working for the upliftment of the poor in rural areas of the state. He was tutoring the youth and helped them prepare for higher studies. He also used to teach self-defence to women and girls. Meanwhile, he started writing a book on corruption in the system. It wasn't much, but it was good honest work, and Mahesh was satisfied. Little did he know, a storm was brewing, and soon, he would be at the centre of it.

As expected, *Babuji* won the election by a record margin and rumours were rife that he would be the next CM. One morning, Mahesh got a call from *Babuji's* PA that *Babuji* wanted him to attend the swearing-in ceremony. Mahesh had gotten the news way before the others, confirming the rumours. But what surprised Mahesh the most was that *Babuji* had asked his PA to convey the news. He chose not to dwell on it thinking *Babuji* might be swamped with work. Mahesh and his father attended the swearing-in ceremony, and *Babuji* met them very warmly in front of all the guests. He once again asked Mahesh by whispering in his ear, "Should I keep Home Ministry for you?" Mahesh just touched his feet and walked away with his father.

Months went by, and slowly, news of corruption started warming the columns of the newspapers. There were whispers in the police department about how key districts were being given to openly corrupt officers. On top of that, cross-border drug smuggling had started, descending the state into chaos.

Mahesh was getting impatient. Not only he, but the common people were also getting restless and frustrated. Corruption was again on an uphill climb, and there were no welfare and development schemes floated by the new regime. He tried to refocus but to no avail.

Unable to get any clear answers, he decided to take the bull by the horns and paid an unannounced visit to the CM's office. *Babuji* was away in Delhi, and his PA (Personal Assistant) was behaving uncharacteristically rudely. "Did you even make an appointment before coming?" the PA barked. Mahesh just couldn't control himself and caught him by his collar and boxed his ears. As he beat him, he couldn't stop. All his frustration flowed through his hands onto the PA's face. He drew a sharp breath as he punched him and spat, "tell me what is happening here? Is it true that corruption corroding the state from within is government-sponsored? Who is behind the smuggling? Who is running the show?" He looked at the PA square in his eyes and demanded, "Tell me, or I will kill you."

Mahesh was pressing on the PA's neck, and after some time, the PA blurted, "Stop, please stop, or I will die. Please. I will tell you everything." Over the next fifteen minutes, the PA spilt the truth about the devil in sheep's clothing. About the man, Mahesh had thought to be an angel. As the PA spoke, Mahesh tried to connect the dots, and the revelation nearly shook the ground from beneath his feet. When everything became crystal clear to him, he was no longer angry. He was livid.

A wild look plastered across Mahesh's face. He felt deceived and betrayed. *Babuji* had political ambitions right from the beginning. His anti-corruption movement was but a front for his nefarious activities. It was never about the welfare of the society, but to increase his popularity with the people. He used Mahesh to destroy the network of the previous CM and replaced it with his network.

Brilliant—… Mahesh thought, about how easily *Babuji* fooled the entire state and even him.

He decided to pay a visit to *Babuji* once he returned from Delhi, where he had gone to invite the Prime Minister to inaugurate an airport in the border district of the state.

Meanwhile, one of his batch mates, who was heading the Intelligence network of the state, called him and asked him to immediately come to his office. As soon as Mahesh reached his office, the friend made him listen to cross-border chatter, where they had intercepted a few calls that were linked to *Babuji*. The CM was heard saying, "I am going to invite him; the rest is up to you and your team." What was even more shocking was the voice on the other end of the call. Someone who was clearly from across the border replied, "You just call him; the rest is all planned. Ab Dilli door nahin." Loosely translated as "The Prime Minister's seat is not far." This was the last missing piece of the puzzle.

Mahesh turned white with shock. Not only were *Babuji's* political ambitions revealed, but the fact that he was the kingpin at the centre of the corruption and smuggling in the country was completely appalling. What was worse was that this was not just national anymore. It was a real shocker to know that *Babuji* was hand-in-hand with foreign powers to eliminate the PM.

As soon as Mahesh heard that *Babuji* was back from Delhi, he rushed to *Babuji's* residence. Pushing aside the guards, dashing through the security cordon, he rushed straight towards the bedroom. Mahesh pulled *Babuji* from his bed and threw him down on the ground, "You. You are the most awful and cunning person I have ever known, a traitor of the highest order. With all the lives you've destroyed with your horrible plans, you don't deserve to live."

Before *Babuji* could even utter a word, Mahesh pointed his revolver at his temple. With bloodshot eyes, he looked straight at *Babuji*, who was too stunned to respond. The security guards entered the room, and a scuffle enthused. One of the guards fired at Mahesh. The bullet missed him by a whisker, but in that melee, Mahesh's revolver went off and struck *Babuji*. He died on the spot. The police arrived soon after and arrested Mahesh.

Driving away in the police van, thinking of his past glory, Mahesh was unaware of just how he had forever changed the course of the country's politics. With the news of *Babuji's* passing, the news about his involvement with traitors too spread like wildfire. The sensational news swept the nation about how a sitting CM was involved in a conspiracy to assassinate the PM in partnership with the enemy country. All credibility was lost, and the countrymen looked up to Mahesh as a hero.

Mahesh's arrest was strongly opposed, and the clamour for Mahesh's release kept on spreading and increasing by the day. The entire state came to a standstill as protests swept the state. The government was left with no other option but to approach the courts for Mahesh's release.

Shortly, Mahesh walked out of the prison and thanked the people of the state who fought for his release. He resumed his work at the NGO, vowing never to fall for another conniving bastard again. Ultimately, truth and good always prevail, and he finished his book on corruption in the system, which to no one's surprise, instantly became a bestseller.

My Life, My Way

Neeta Ranbhan

It all started very slowly. Repeated stiff neck due to looking under a microscope in degree college and subsequently followed by severe muscle and joint pain.

The Doctors just prescribed some painkillers and said exertion may be the cause but tests and radiographs later confirmed and gave a name to my malady... I was suffering from "Ankylosing spondylitis", which is an auto-immune incurable disease but not at all life-threatening.

The mobility of the patient gets compromised. Pain and stiffness, and deformity in joints are the symptoms. The Doctors were not worried much as this was not a life-threatening disease.

For me, the struggle was overcoming the pain, the constant aggravation of a stiff neck. Lifestyle changes happened. Everything changed over the years.... the suffering would ebb and flow but was there, always lurking somewhere in the background. Life continued, somewhat slower maybe, and most definitely not the way I had planned it.

Then a further blow struck. One day suddenly, I lost the movement of my right hip joint. I couldn't get up from bed or fold my leg to sit cross-legged. It was excruciatingly painful to even move that leg. My family members became overprotective. I learnt to hide my pain from them, lest they just hover over me like bees over flowers and insist that I stay in bed all day long. The idea of bed rest was too vile even to contemplate. I could see my life coming to a complete standstill, and I lived in the mortal fear of how I would cope with it if that were really to happen. Imagine not going out, not breathing in the fresh morning air, not sitting out with your loved ones in warm dusky evenings, not going shopping, not meeting friends? No movie night? No random dinners? Oh no!

What if I am kept in a room like an invalid, and personal maids or nurses get appointed to take care of me? I could see my life slipping away from me like sand particles drifting in the breeze.

Then, just as I was despairing, came my Eureka moment!

When a calamity falls on us, God also slowly opens a window for a sliver of light to come in. He shows us a path to follow, and it is up to us to seize that opportunity. I decided that neither did I want a life of an invalid when I was just thirty-eight years of age, nor would I like people sympathising with me—I hate pity—so I took hold of the reins of my life in my hands and vowed to live on my own terms. First things first, I learnt to hide the fact that I was suffering when in public. I put on a brave face and made little of my pain and disability.

The Doctor said now only surgery might bring back my movements. But again, he warned this is a disease involving all joints, so he left me to work on it with alternative therapies.

He gave me three months. It was either the surgery (which I dreaded!) or my determination to overcome it with alternative medicines and lifestyle changes. Yes, you guessed it right! I chose not to go under a knife. His words, "Either you try out various therapies and continue limping, or you come back for surgery," spurred me to turn to alternative medicines even faster. I had to try everything possible before I even contemplated back or hip surgery and going under anaesthesia.

Of course, I never went back for surgery.

This is where my real mission to take care of my health started. Over the years, I did not leave a stone unturned to fight with my condition.

A multidisciplinary approach was necessary, so first and foremost, I started with Yoga. Simple *asanas* and *pranayama* began my day. I employed a yoga teacher who, with her gentle hands and steady instructions, made me do stretching and asanas. Slowly we progressed to doing more difficult ones. To my immense astonishment, I could manoeuvre my body and attempt different asanas.

I also started meditating. I had never believed in the power of meditation till then, but faith in the divine and surrender to the almighty helped me achieve a sense of peace and stability. I turned to all branches of alternative therapies like Homeopathy, Naturopathy, and Ayurveda, not leaving any stone unturned in my quest for a cure. Yes, it helped…some things were picked up from Naturopathy, some from Ayurveda, etc., but what helped was my basic trust and an instinct in what to follow. A proper diet, exercise, and a good night's sleep added to my healing.

I did it all, taking it up as a challenge and with one thing in mind—God has given me an illness that was not life-threatening, so I thought his message was clear enough for me to fight and win.

What I have learnt from my journey is never to give up in life. My message to all who are fighting some health issue or other is that keep on trying; success will come your way! If life is there, then rest assured and have faith that you will overcome your illness.

Be strong, and for that, take all help available. Surrender and keep the faith. Make yoga and meditation, Satsang, and *sewa* (devotion) your mainstay, along with all the prescribed medications.

Try to prove to yourself that you are as good as any healthy person and take it up as a challenge. I have learnt to do things like any normal person—taking care of my family, my home, and my near ones. I also practice Dentistry (I am a dentist by profession) and do many activities of social service in the Inner wheel club. I am a teacher at the AOL (Art of Living) Foundation. I travel a lot, and in fact, I am always in a hurry to do everything now and live in the present moment.

Sometimes I feel my illness has made me into a better person, so should I just take it as a blessing in disguise? Oh yes! Most definitely, don't you think?

To the Stars and Back

Shirley Verghese

She was in severe pain. Her back had given up several times at different spots. Sometimes it was the neck. At other times her lower back or the tailbone. There was hardly any respite from the shooting spasms that brought tears of frustration and acute pain simultaneously to her sad eyes.

Gone were the days when all that occupied her mind and days were burning issues that keep her organisation going. She now spent hours reminiscing about those hectic days when hundreds of helpless people in the community looked to her for support, guidance, and redemption from their daily struggles for a dignified livelihood.

Amala would wake up every morning with fresh ideas flowing out of her frontal lobes as she inhaled the strong aroma of her black coffee. She had to leave before 9 a.m. to wade through the traffic to reach her workplace, twenty-three km away on the outskirts of the city. It was a perpetual struggle for her to put the house in order, organise the cleaning and cooking for the day, sending her daughter Mansi to school before she ventured out for the day. Evening duties rested with her husband Rizwan, who would be around when the child was back from school. That was an unspoken arrangement when they decided to start a family.

*****

Amala came from a simple middle-class South Indian family with two siblings. She was the delicate one who got more attention, whereas her elder sister and younger brother were less pampered. Nothing exciting or eventful to cherish from her childhood stood out in her memory, except for a devoted mother and a harassed father who had more worries than joys. Burdened with the heavy workload at his factory and preoccupied with sustaining his family; he was a hardly cheerful and approachable father figure.

Amala was close to her elder sister. She was the only one she could share her fears, her dreams, and longings. She really had no close friends at school. But she stood apart with this wild streak of independence, of making choices early in life, unlike her sister, who always succumbed to parental expectations and pressures. In college, she took to studying arts for graduation and later chose a rather unheard career in social work. Her parents were perplexed and had no clue how to rein her into their expectations. They were often bewildered by her comings and goings, her interacting with people who had never figured on their horizon of normal people. Soon, she joined an NGO (Non-Governmental Organisation) that focused on social issues of education, empowerment, and health for economically weaker urban sections. They mainly comprised daily wage earners, small vendors, mill workers, unskilled labourers, and their families living in less developed areas of the city.

That strong-willed child had ventured on the untrodden path; her decided path. Becoming aware of her dreams and idea of *'becoming someone with a purpose to make a difference to the world at large.'* She was charged with the power to pursue that journey to the stars. It was a lofty and idealistic goal for a young graduate out of college, ready to conquer the world. She was already well-read in literature, sociology, and history to be aware of larger issues that chased humanity and resulted in victimisation and imbalances in social structures. She was disturbed and confused at the widening gaps between the 'well-to-dos' and the lesser beings; how they all lived and breathed together on this very earth in their diversities.

In her impressionable age, these were issues that formed part of her living in two distinct compartments. In the company of her friends and colleagues, she was an animated and passionate campaigner for relevant causes and pursued to find their remedies like any young warrior. At home, she would be lost in her thoughts and sealed her lips about such ideas and thoughts, which perhaps would never meet the approval or appreciation of her parents.

She was lonely but scared to admit it. However, her demeanour was always of a confident, carefree, and happy person. She longed to lean on someone who trusted her, but she could never let go until she was sure of herself. The young men who found her attractive and pursued her for long-term commitments found her unyielding. They were too immature for her and were far from her utopian dreams of being a *'change maker.'*

The heart has a way of flipping at the most vulnerable moments of one's life. She was disturbed that it was happening to her. In the middle of the slums and groups of semi-literate women and children whose lives were being re-charted with her support, something was happening within the deep chambers of her emotions. Her mentor was a dedicated medical professional who had already planned how the organisation would meet the challenges and needs of the community they had chosen to work with. Development in any area had to focus on its elementary roots—education, health, and economic stability. There were social issues of women empowerment, violence, and poverty.

Amala had never seen nor experienced life beyond her secure home. It was a shocking transformation as she quickly slipped into the action mode of working hands-on with people who could not respond, understand, or want to make shifts in their ways of thinking and living. It was as if they had already resigned to their fate, with no scope of believing that life could be better for them.

Days passed into months and years later, and she found herself drawn completely into the world of a changing community. The 'utopian dream' was coming alive amidst the squalor and grit of crowds that gathered around them, listening and following the difficult path of elevating themselves to better health, knowledge, and new-found confidence in meeting their own challenges. This was more satisfying than being amongst her college friends, who by then had found life partners, great careers, and secure jobs with a steady income. She remained content with her allowance for subsistence as fixed by the funding agencies.

Proximity with colleagues at the workplace builds lasting bonds, especially when one follows a person who seems totally dedicated, convinced, and committed to a noble cause. Amala did not realise that she had unknowingly covered her path in the footsteps of Dr. Rizwan all along her journey. Apparently, they were on the same road that 'destiny' had marked out. She was conscious that she could not find another man with her vision and mission. Their lives were getting entwined with one another, as she was spending all her wakeful hours with him.

This was despite the growing awareness that apart from their idealism and commitment to a common cause, they were completely different in personality, their attitudes, family background, and outlook on life. And yet, she was so drawn to him that she was willing to make a complete makeover unconditionally. It only happens to a headstrong youngster willing to throw all caution to the wind and take a leap of faith. The ability to weigh the practical aspects of the consequence of such a huge allegiance to a cause to an individual eluded her at that time.

There were other complications to deal with. She wanted to marry a man ten years older, someone from another community and who was already a father of a five-year-old child. Dr. Rizwan was rather sceptical, but he could hardly resist his own deep attraction to this gorgeous woman of his dreams. Amala, however, was able to deal with that situation and urged him to get a legal clearance for them to get married. It was a big decision to convey to her parents. She was not faint-hearted.

She dared to confront them one day which they found very hard to accept. "But, Dad, I like Rizwan and will be happy with him," fell on deaf ears. So, she felt compelled to walk out of the comfort and warmth of her close-knit family, to follow her man, for better or for worse, to build a life on their own terms. Only she knew the price she had to pay for what her head and heart truly wanted.

"Don't worry, darling, they will come around. Give them some time," Rizwan reasoned with her, whenever he saw her unhappy.

"But why can't they understand and accept their daughter's choice?" she asked him repeatedly.

"Have patience! I promise things will fall in place; Rizwan assured her. You are walking the untrodden path once again against society, family, and friends who find it hard to accept your decision. Think from their point of view. Nobody in your family had dared to walk this path."

Time has a way of healing deep wounds. It was not long before Amala and Rizwan were welcome to her parent's home.... by a typical cliché. They became grandparents to a beautiful granddaughter, Mansi! Happy times prevailed.

There were many NGOs working in the field to create awareness, maintain peace and harmony. For Amala and Rizwan, the work which started as a passion and dream became a compelling career that demanded every ounce of their physical and mental energy. From managing the funding for the growing activities of the organisation to the training needs of grass root workers and hiring professional help to run the office and accounts, the responsibilities kept increasing. There were moments of satisfaction looking back at their achievements, recognition of their contribution to society, and the change in the quality of lives of the communities they worked in over the past three decades.

Invitations to national and international forums helped to showcase their work, picking up issues and highlighting the need for inclusion in the governing bodies, especially regarding the legal rights of women and their place in society, be it education, employment, or equal opportunities. Amala was a known face and respected voice among social activists by the time she touched her fifties.

Financially they were unable to save for their rainy days on their meagre salaries. But then, it never bothered her until one day, she realised that she had a grown-up daughter who had her needs too. Her own health issues needed serious medical attention. They had not even invested in buying a house for themselves. Retirement had not occurred to either of them!

Amala started feeling the burden and suddenly wondered if her approach to life and her path was making her insecure. The anxiety of fighting the policies for availing of foreign funds for social causes and managing to garner funds to run the organisations and staff kept her preoccupied. By then, she had her own registered wing of activities exclusively for the welfare of women.

All of it took a toll on her fragile health, and she was finding it hard to cope physically. It took a while for her to realise that she had perhaps reached the end of her road. "*Thus far and no more*" was beginning to fill her awareness. It was a painful decision that could not be prolonged any further. Her friends and close family encouraged her to slow down and devote time to herself and focus on dealing with her personal well-being.

Hanging on to the edge of reality, Amala found herself abruptly landing on ground zero with a thud. She wondered what the decades behind her meant. She wondered where she figured out the flurry of missions to be accomplished. She found it hard to let go of her daughter Mansi, who wanted to go abroad to complete specialisation in the area of her interest in fine arts. Having endured the struggles with her parents, Mansi had a different view of what she wanted to do. Perhaps, she would want to change her career and not pursue the work started by them.

"Why don't you ever voice your opinion? Why are you always so silent? Always just observing? You Know, Mansi wants to go abroad for further studies, how are we going to finance her?" Amala's questions went unanswered whenever she confronted her husband. Rizwan would just smile through his glasses with an indulgent look at his wife and continue reading or writing his diary.

*****

Time has a way of toning down everything. Life teaches us to handle accolades and brick bats, failures, and disappointments with a stoic mind. Rizwan had turned inwards somewhere along the way. He was a man of few words. Unlike her, who voiced and aired every thought that brewed in her head, he preferred to stay silent. One could never figure out if he was happy or sad, or indifferent. He was a person who just did what he had to do. Results and consequences were beside the point for him. He would never engage with Amala on any issue and allow it to end in discord. He would gently remind her to be mindful of her health and remain calm when she would get worked up.

Amala spent her time musing and ruminating about everything that happened in her life, from the time she left home to this stage of vacant solitude. Sometimes she wondered if her journey was worth all the struggle and sacrifice. She did not have any tangible assets to flaunt or lean upon. She did have a good set of friends who were there when needed, but it was not in her to ask for help! Her old colleagues in the field would occasionally connect and reminisce about their good times at work. Sometimes, she would be invited to chair meetings or give a talk about her experience in the field. Those were joyous moments for her.

For someone who dared to be different and stand apart from the milling crowds of people who just lived for themselves, Amala was indeed a shining star who broke all the typical conventions to prove her worth and dream of making a difference in the lives of hundreds of people.

Amala had walked on faithfully on the road never travelled, and she was happy that she had set out to be a trailblazer for many to follow her. She opened her diary and re-read the poem that never failed to fascinate her, which by now she knew by heart–

Casabianca

"The boy stood on the burning deck,

Whence all but he had fled;

The flame that lit the battle's wreck,

Shone round him o'er the dead.

Yet beautiful and bright he stood,

As born to rule the storm;

A creature of heroic blood,

A proud, though childlike form."

–Felicia Hemans

She closed her diary and turned towards Rizwan. He was lost in a deep sleep, a sleep of an innocent and carefree baby. She switched off her bedside lamp and drew the warm comforter around her aching body. Smiling to herself, she let out a contented sigh; after all, she had lived life on her own terms and lived it well!

Trailing the Forbidden Lane

Binta Elsa Biju

'Be on the right track,'
Life often mutters at the
so-called turning points.
But, it only ends me in a
state of utter confusion and
chaos.
What is essentially the resonating
view of 'right' track?
I've seen many footprints
imprinted on that ideal track.
Some seem to be faded
over the years, while
others are no longer there,
as they get vanished
out of sight and mind by
the arrival of new imprints.

Then also, the mind murmurs,
'Be on the right track—as
it is what others anticipate from me
still leaving me disparagingly
perplexed.
Finally, my 'self' dares to
step of the comfort zone
to assert my true self.

Because I want my footprints to
remain unique; not
shrouded by several others.
At last, I decide to make
a move in the
less trodden path—
Firmly believing it as
my life's 'right' track.

A Head Screwed on Wrong!!

Col Gaurav Bhatia, PhD (Retd)

"What would life be if we had no courage to attempt anything?"

–Vincent van Gogh

The Road Not Taken

"I came on earth for something, I must do something, and I must live and leave not just anything but something!"

–Ernest Agyemang Yeboah

These seminal words have grown on me, and I have adopted them as my life's ethos. Whether it is something as mundane as choosing an ice cream flavour or helping my wife select the colour of her nail paint, or deciding on a strategy to tackle a work-related challenge, the one theme that has been cross-cutting across all my decision cliffs mirrors what Robert Frost wrote in his world-famous poem **"The Road Not Taken"**—

Two roads diverged in a wood, and I took the one less travelled,
And that has made all the difference.

Feeling Anxious on The Road Not Taken

"As the world we live in is so unpredictable, the ability to learn and adapt to change is imperative, alongside creativity, problem-solving, and communication skills."

–Alain Dehaze

Eighteen years after commissioning in the Indian Army, I finally took over as Commandant of my Regiment in 2008. The task of monitoring the welfare of 600-plus troops felt supremely exciting—a little unnerving too. It seemed to instantly inject me with a heightened sense of responsibility. The commencement of a new journey in the absence of any precedence to guide my actions called for both courage and determination.

I firmly believe that a positive mental frame, a small leap of faith, and an unwavering trust in God equip us with the ability to use an unfamiliar situation to our advantage. It also enables us to progress unhindered on the road less travelled—towards novel experiences, unexpected results, and myriad fortunes.

The first thing I noticed upon my joining was the *cobwebs of status quo* that hung in the air around me. Two decades of blind adherence to unquestioned traditions and a lack of precedence for attempting anything new seemed to have crystallised these cobwebs. I knew it was time to *break the status quo* and tread the *Untrodden Path* to add value to the Regiment. The To-Do list was long spanning multiple institutions/activities, but top on my priority scale were the *Barber Shop, the Baṛā Khānā, and the Sarva Dharma Sthal (SDS) Parade.*

Let me take my readers on a rapid time-telescoped journey through my professional voyage and narrate a few instances that exemplify my life ethos of always trying to paddle up the *Untrodden Creak (Path).*

The "Fear Naught" Barbers Shop

Exemplary uniformity, fastidious discipline, and being consistently smart are the sine qua non of a soldier in the Army. All of this starts with being taught the axiom of *Right Place, Right Time, Right Dress*[1] —always and every time. The Fear Naughts' (*soldiers, JCO and officers of 50 Armoured Regiment*) were no different and everyone who sported the "Red & Green"[2] and swore allegiance to being a "Digvijay"[3] warrior adhered to these tenets.

To maintain the uniformity and discipline of all members of the Regiment, especially with respect to the haircut *(Crew cut or Katora cut—as it is colloquially called*), an important institution of the Regiment is the Barber Shop. Nearly everyone would visit the Barber Shop at least once every fortnight, if not sooner. The steady stream of soldiers, JCOs, and officers seeking a haircut maintained a steady footfall in the Barbers Shop and kept the Barbers engaged 24x7x365.

---

[1] Colloquial phrase – As per the author conscientiously following this axiom while in the Armed Forces, saves one from being ticked off on frivolous issues of dress, turnout, timeliness etc.

[2] Red & Green – Colours of the Regiment. In the strict martial sense, these colours when seen in unison depict the traditional Verey Light success signal of "Red over Green" which signifies victory in battle. In a generic sense, Red is the traditional cavalry colour signifying supreme sacrifice while Green stands for the basic desire for peace, harmony, and wellbeing of all ranks of the regiment. Seen together, the colours signify the regiment's preparation for the supreme sacrifice when called upon to do so, from a basic stance of peace, harmony, and well-being. These colours adorn the flag of the regiment.

[3] Motto of 50 Armoured Regiment – दिग्विजय : Digvijay *"Victory in All Directions and Planes, in War and in Peace"*.

Right from my commissioning in 1990, one had visited this institution many times and had come to accept the less than savoury/congenial conditions of the Barber Shop as *de riguer.*

A resolve to make a significant improvement to this institution got us thinking. My key partners in this initiative were Lt Col Arvind Verma, Second in Command & Risaldar Major Kashmira Singh, and Risaldar Major.

The desire to make a sea change to this institution started with selecting a large hall near the barracks, followed by installing a hydraulically operated entrance door, getting the premises professionally painted with textured paint, panelling the walls with huge full-length mirrors, procuring four *state-of-the-art* Maddox Professional Barber Chairs along with professional quality electronically operated shavers and high quality manually operated barber implements.

The acid test came when we decided to make the Barber Shop completely air-conditioned, but due to limited financial resources available at my disposal, a choice had to be made between installing one AC in my office and another one in the Officers' Mess Guest Room or getting both the AC's installed in the Barber Shop. It was a no-brainer; the *Untrodden Path* was clear. The Barber Shop won, hands down. Together we succeeded in creating the first fully airconditioned Barber Shop for the troops in the history of the Armoured Corps and provided them with a *Luxe Salon* experience within the confines of the cantonment in the Regimental precinct.

A Special "Baṛā Khānā"[1] for the Tradesmen[2]

The organisation of a Baṛā Khānā is an occasion for merriment for all ranks, but every such occasion translates to additional work for the Tradesmen since they are the primary manpower who toils silently behind the scenes to provide the entire wherewithal for the successful conduct of the Baṛā Khānā.

"It is only with the heart that one can see rightly; what is essential is (often) invisible to the eye."

–Antoine de Saint-Exupery

These words struck me as completely true with respect to this anecdote. I served in my Regiment for nearly two decades before being anointed as the Commandant. I do not exactly remember, but I must have attended at least a hundred plus *Baṛā Khānā's* with the troops, and the flaw in the system completely escaped my attention. As I attended the Republic Day *Baṛā Khānā* in 2009, my heart saw what was invisible to the eye—*in fact, it had been for two decades.*

So, what was it that I had missed all my life?

I had completely ignored and glossed over the fact that the Tradesmen never get to attend a *Baṛā Khānā.* Whenever such an occasion is planned, this army of silent workers is always performing

---

[1] Baṛā Khānā – a special meal wherein all ranks (soldiers/JCOs/Officers) dine together in a relaxed atmosphere of mutual bonhomie. This is aimed at raising the morale of troops by providing them proximity with the officers, who normally have a separate dining arrangement in the Officers' Mess.

[2] A unit in the Army is a completely self-dependent, self-sustaining microcosm with availability of soldiers proficient in various non-martial trades, these are as varied as Chef, Hairdresser, Store Hand, Animal Store Holders, Ferrier, Pioneers, Postal, Steward, Artisan (Wood), Artisan (Painter), Artisan (Tailor), Artisan (Metallurgy), Artisan (Musician), Equipment Repairer, Kennel Man, Washer man, Mess Keeper and the Housekeeper.

behind the scenes—either planning, preparing, executing, serving, or clearing up—before/during/after the event.

How could I have missed this fact? I was mentally kicking myself and feeling guilty and sheepish at the same time. Amends had to be made—and I got into a huddle with my *trusted duo sounding board*—the Second-in-Command and the Risaldar Major. They concurred with my observation, and we decided to create a new institution of a quarterly *Tradesmen's Special Baṛā Khānā.*

"Creativity is thinking up new things.
Innovation is doing new things."

–Theodore Levitt

This resolve eventually translated to the Tradesmen being left completely free for half a day. That particular meal for the other personnel of the Regiment was prepared under crew cooking arrangements by all ranks, less the Tradesmen. All the Tradesmen were made to feel special, thanked for their continued service to the Regiment, and treated to a *Thali* meal procured ex-trade *(Pehelwan Da Dhaba).*

The most telling comment I received as we wound up the first such Tradesmen's Special *Baṛā Khānā* was from one of the affected Tradesmen, who with moist eyes stated—*"Sahab, mujhe 27 saal ho gaye fauj mein—ur yeh pahla Baṛā Khānā hai jo maine tassalli se baith kar enjoy kiya hai."* (Sir, I have been in the Army for twenty-seven years, and this is the first time that I have enjoyed this meal heartily).

All the guilt and embarrassment that I had experienced at having missed out on this important aspect of welfare for two decades—

started to slowly dissipate as we together stepped onto another Untrodden Path.

The "Sarva Dharma Sthal (SDS)" Parade[1]

Army life is scrupulously secular.

The Commanding Officer *(Commandant in the case of an Armoured Regiment)* of a unit is responsible for the religious and spiritual well-being of his *jawans*. Depending on the class composition, a unit can have a Mandir, Gurudwara, Church or Mosque, or all these together. Designated Unit Pandit, Granthi, Priest, or Maulvi are specially trained to impart religious teaching with due respect to all religions, and they also maintain the unit's religious institutes and conduct various rituals and functions. In an *All India—All Class mixed unit*, rather than having separate religious places, a *Sarva Dharma Sthal* (common prayer hall) is provided, where all troops meet for various religious functions. All ranks, irrespective of their religion, attend and take an active part in the festivals of all religions represented in a unit. In the case of our Regiment, every Sunday, the whole unit had gathered, since being raised in 1990—to attend the weekly religious prayers or the SDS Parade as it was referred to.

With this backdrop, I bring you a casual interaction I had with a Khalsa soldier from my Regiment while I was commanding my Regiment from 2008-2010. His simplistic query was—"*Sahab Ji, Sunday ko SDS Parade mein aane ke chakkar mein "kesh" nahin dho paate. Late ho jata hai. Kya ham SDS Parade kisi aur din shaam ko nahin kar sakte?* (Sir, we cannot wash our hair on Sunday morning as we must be present for the SDS parade. Can't we keep this parade in an evening?).

Though the buck finally stops at the Commandant, most

---

[1] http://www.indiandefencereview.com/spotlights/a-glimpse-of-life-in-the-army/2/

administrative decisions in the microcosm of a Cavalry Regiment are largely democratic. I am usually not one who dithers while taking a decision, but the fact that on hand was a two-decade-old precedence, I was conservatively cautious—lest I end up missing the forest for the trees. The request appeared straightforward, simplistic, and logical. Though it came from one individual soldier, I realised that this would probably be a common problem for other soldiers / JCOs in the Regiment too.

"*The Three Musketeers*" (Second-in-Command/Risaldar Major and I), along with the other officers and JCOs of the Regiment, went back to the drawing board to resolve this predicament. The fact that this journey might lead me up another *Untrodden Path*—was not lost on me. The decision essentially was to shift the SDS Parade from Sunday morning to any other day—preferably in the evening. While we were battling with this imbroglio, I was reminded of another imponderable connection to the SDS, which had been identified a few weeks ago by my wife, Ranju. Her observation *(read-objection)* lay with the system by which *Prasad* was prepared in weekly rotation by each Squadron Langar for distribution after the prayers, being cooked in the same cooking utensils, in which, in all probability, other non-vegetarian food items, etc. had also been prepared.

I decided to tackle both these aspects in one fell swoop. Based on concurrence from all concerned, including the Regiment Panditji—two *Untrodden Paths* were traversed together. Firstly, the SDS Parade was shifted from Sunday morning to Tuesday evening, and secondly, a new set of utensils *(Kadahi, Palta, etc.)* for cooking only the Prasad were procured from the Quartermaster store and handed over to the Regiment Panditji. The responsibility of the four squadrons to provide the ingredients and the manpower for the preparation of the prasad, however, remained unchanged.

The "PCPP" (Passion Converts Pressure to Pleasure) Principle

The sum of our education, experiences, and the resultant skill sets is what propels us ahead in our life journeys. The challenges that we encounter and the way we tackle them—decide whether one would be counted as a *"winner", an "also-ran," or a "loser."* Given a choice, all of us would like to think that we deserve to be counted among the members of the first cohort, but often in our hearts of hearts, one knows that we ought to be in the second or the third cohort.

This thought coalesces well with a statement that I heard Kapil Dev, the cricketer makes in a public gathering. He opined that whether it is children or grown-ups, professionals or homemakers, males or females—the people of this world today, in general, are increasingly feeling *"under pressure/pressured/pressurised."* The simplistic answer he suggests to this imbroglio is to let your *"Passion—Convert Pressure to Pleasure (PCPP Principle)."*

This seamlessly gels with the age-old wisdom shared many moons ago by Marc Anthony—

"If you do what you love, you'll never work a day in your life."

–Marc Anthony

This has been my guiding principle in life, and I have attempted to remain positive, upbeat, driven, and motivated all through the five-plus decades of my existence on this "*blue marble*". I make a conscious effort to thrive by dint of my passion for excelling in whatever God guides me towards, and that allows me the liberty of obviating any pressure points. On the contrary, I try and convert them into a pleasurable peregrination of traversing new and hitherto uncharted territory—the multitude of *Untrodden Paths* of my life's journey.

"I have my own unique road that has had many exciting ups and heart-breaking downs, but one thing I know is that my journey is not

over, and the best is yet to come."

–Ryan Hall

Paradise Lost

Vaishali Chandorkar Chitale

Sheila was a homemaker. Coming from an affluent family and married into one, she had never felt the need to work, per se, for money.

She was an interior designer and worked for herself. She loved her work, and was good at it, as was evident from the home she had created for them when they had bought this duplex in the upmarket area of the city. She had also done up her friends' houses at their request and loved her work.

Her husband Anand, a chartered accountant, had his own practice. True to his name, he was 'happy-go-lucky' and rarely let anything get him down and tread through murky waters on light feet. Nothing ever perturbed him, and she had marvelled at his proclivity for brushing off the disquieting under the carpet. She thanked God that their two sons—Aarav,15, and Sachiv,12 had not just inherited his happy nature but were also hardworking and determined like her.

Life was good, that is, if you count the fact that they had a good home to live in, children were enrolled in exclusive private schools, there was money for an occasional holiday abroad and basic necessities and more were looked into by the 'man of the house,' so to say!

Sheila envisioned her life to cruise along this path, smooth and steady, with maybe a minor bump or two coming their way; for which she was well prepared! After all, life is never perfect; she knew that very well. Being an optimist, she never worried about things, not in her control. Glancing into her future, she saw children grown up, and settled in their careers; Anand and she secure financially, in good health, enjoying retirement, travelling, and spending time with their grandchildren. Of course, all that was still a far way off, but dream she could!

But then, life has a way of throwing a curved ball, when least expected!

It all started during Diwali of that year. Like any Indian household, Diwali meant merriment, good food, laughter, fun, new clothes, fairy lights, *diyas*, gifts for everyone—sometimes a piece or two of jewellery for her—and happy days. She liked to start her preparations a week before, getting the *diyas* ready with their wicks immersed in oil for smooth lighting on the D day, setting up the fairy lights on the balconies and inside the house, she loved draping some lights around the windows from inside, to give a festive look; buying new clothes for the boys, her gift from Anand and of course preparing the delicacies which were enjoyed by all. Diwali also meant the extended family (her parents, his parents, and his sister's family) gathering at their place on *Laxmi Puja* (prayers to Hindu Goddess Laxmi) with 'pot-luck' dinner to follow before breaking off for the day.

So, as usual, on that bustling morning, she had gone to their guest room cupboard to open the safe in which they kept their silver *'Ganesha and Laxmi'* (Hindu Gods) idols, silver *thalis*, small bowls, glasses, utensils, cutlery, *diyas*, etc. She liked cleaning them a few days before so that there was never a last-minute hitch. A meticulous planner, she liked being prepared rather than rushing around at the last minute.

Humming to herself, she had opened the safe, visualizing the things she needed to retrieve and clean. The safe had opened soundlessly and revealed its contents. A sense of foreboding took hold of her. She gaped at the open safe as if in a trance. A compartment that was chock-a-block with silver and jewellery, had only some spoons, small *diyas*, and other sundry items lying around haphazardly. Too stunned to react, she had stood staring at the contents. She had started shivering in her fright. The first thought was theft. She remembered screaming out Anand's name in a funny high-pitched voice. Anand and both the boys had come running. A shocked silence followed. She had turned to Anand, deep in despair, wailing. He had held her, sat her down, and consoled her. A sense of urgency had taken hold of her. She got up as if to call the police, to report the robbery, but Anand kept pushing her down, to sit, to have water.

"Anand, we need to call the police! We have to report this. Oh God! When did this happen? How come we never came to know? How come nothing else was stolen?" thoughts bubbled out of her.

"Sit down, Sheila, calm down."

"Calm down! Calm? Anand, do you even know what you are saying? How can you be calm? All our silver is gone… my jewellery…"

By this time, the boys had retrieved her jewellery cases, and as expected, they were empty. She was devastated and cried out in anguish.

Her mind was ticking. Who could have done this? The house help? No, they never left the house to servants. Her morning cook? No, not possible; she always came before Sheila left for work. Dhobi? No, he had never been to the guest room. Watchmen of the building? Impossible, they were trustworthy. Then who?

"Oh, God! Oh God! Diwali is within a week. Oh God! How will we manage? Anand, go to the police station and get the cops. We have to report this. Meanwhile, I am calling our parents," the planner in her took over.

She had almost pushed Anand out of the house, surprised at his reluctance to go. Thinking nothing of it, she had instructed the children not to touch anything and called her parents. Her shivering had abated by then as children hovered around her, unusually quiet for them.

Her mind was working furiously. Ok, so they had lost their silver… some of her earrings and small neck pieces. Thank God, most of her jewellery was in the bank's locker… Diwali was around the corner… both sets of parents as guests… silver was needed for the Puja… what could be done? How to go about it now? She had sat there deep in thought, absentmindedly chewing her nails.

By the time the cops had left, she had been ready with an alternate plan. Parents had rallied around. It was decided that some basic silver things like the big *diya*, a *thali*, and two small bowls should be bought immediately for Diwali and let the police do their work and catch the thieves. All hoped, though were doubtful whether they would get all the stolen goods back.

*****

After a restless night, she had gone to the bank the next day. Her mother had insisted on accompanying her. A feeling of déjà vu enveloped her as she saw the cashier approaching her; her expression unreadable… a little embarrassed?... a bit perplexed?... sheepish?

"Ma'am, I am sorry, but your account has insufficient funds."

"How's that possible? I rarely withdraw money from this account," she quavered.

"Hmmmm… why don't we check the statement?"

They trooped to the manager's office. A sense of foreboding

wrapped around her. The screen blinked, and her account details flashed before them. She squinted at the numbers displayed on the screen. Something was wrong. Very wrong. Only Rs. 2654/-? How?? She shook her head and looked at her mother in confusion.

"Huuhhhhh…how's that possible? I had over six lakhs here… where's all the money gone?" she spluttered, absolutely stunned.

The manager opened another page and was scrutinizing its contents.

"You have withdrawn money at least three times this month only… last month you withdrew Rs…"

"No, no... I have not withdrawn anything… when did I withdraw? How much did I withdraw? I haven't been to the bank for ages…"

"Your husband had come with a signed cheque, Ma'am… I remember… he had come to my cabin as the amount was rather large and we wanted to know how he wanted it… i.e. in bundles of 500 or 100?"

She had sunk down on the chair as her legs gave away. Her mother held her close and tried to make sense of what was happening. The manager took in the scene and immediately called for water and a printout of the statement. She had ordered the cheques which had been cashed to be brought to her.

A total of ten cheques were shown to them. He had over a period of six months, withdrawn small amounts so as not to raise any doubts, except for a large amount of 1.75 lakhs. All the cheques had her signature. Too stunned to take in the enormity of the situation, she had flopped back in her chair, confused and frightened. Everything was a blur…

She didn't remember the ride back home and being led to her room. Raised voices could be heard from the drawing room, though they felt as if coming from far—far away. Her father's angry tone, Anand's smooth voice, her mother's placating tones, his parents... all jumbled up. No sense…

What was the meaning of all this? Where had the money gone? What was Anand's role in this? Had he forged her signature? Was he even capable of such a dastardly act? No… not her Anand, surely? Not the Anand she had known for the last eighteen years! He could have just asked her for the money… But then, why did he even need the money? He was earning well, *wasn't he? WASN'T HE? What was going on?* Thoughts raced through her mind… she shook her head as if to shake off the cobwebs… she must be dreaming… a bad dream… a nightmare from which she will wake up to find the world back to its senses… she would tell Anand while having their morning tea and both will laugh at the silliness of it…

Seemingly, after a lifetime later… but must have been just a couple of hours—her parents came to the room. Their faces were grave. A heavy silence filled the room. Her father took her hand in his. "Sheila…uh… I don't know what to say… Anand owes over 67 lakhs to various agencies… people whom he has borrowed from, and unpaid credit card bills… did you know he had *twenty-five* credit cards?… overdrafts… money borrowed against your FDs, bank loans… it's a mess! How did it come to this? What was he up to? I am totally flummoxed. We need to go about it systematically. I have called my accountant to oversee everything. Do you have your passbooks? Your FD (Fixed Deposit) receipts? We have to check everything… his voice strained.

She had gaped at her father… his words making no sense… *67 lakhs? Why? How?*

Things now started unravelling at a lightning speed. They discovered to their horror that Anand had forged her signature even on their joint FDs, broken the deposits prematurely, and withdrew the amounts. Their post-office savings, done explicitly keeping their children's higher education in mind, were gone too. All their bank accounts had been swept clean.

Why? Why did he need to do this? Slowly the story emerged… Anand had not been earning for some time now. His practice had lagged because he could never deliver on time. He had lost his big clients due to sheer laziness, and others to haphazard ways of working. She always knew he was casual in his approach to life, but even in his work? He had to let go of his staff (which she never knew) because he could not pay their salaries. To her horror, he had no office to go to, he had not renewed the lease… *so where had he been going, when he left the house?*

"Tell me, Anand, what was happening? Where did you go every day? Did you gamble our money away? Did you visit any bars? Tell me… dammit… what did you do with our money?" she screamed at him.

Seeing her anger, he sheepishly confessed, "Sheila, I used to leave home but used to while away the time at our club. To keep up the pretense of earning, I started withdrawing money to run the house."

She gaped at him. "Anand, *what* were you thinking? When did you intend to tell me the truth? You have built a debt of 67 lakhs… 67 LAKHS, Anand! Do you have any idea what you have done? You did not even think of our children! Their future? Oh God! How could I have been so foolish, so trusting?" she berated herself, sinking into the sofa.

He had even mortgaged their house. How? She had not signed any document… but then she remembered…some months back, he had got some legal-looking papers to her—an affidavit—and told her to sign beside his signature, on the crosses marked on all the pages. She had been preoccupied with some household matter… on being asked, he had said nothing important, it was routine; he was renewing the lease of his office rent agreement! She had had no reason to doubt his word, as they used to renew the lease every three years! Oh, God!! What lies!! The scope of his subterfuge amazed her… this was her *husband*!

Something still was not adding up. Besides spending close to 70 lakhs, he had mortgaged the house too, liquidated their deposits, and emptied out their accounts... 67 lakhs was just the tip of the iceberg! Repeated questioning got the same answers. Anand stuck to his story in spite of everyone raising doubts and showing huge potholes in his version of events.

Sheila had reached the end of her tether and was done.

*****

She has filed for divorce and has set about separating her affair—money and otherwise—from his. No alimony wanted (not that he offered), but full custody of children. The house is on the market. She has sold her jewellery and paid off the mortgage. With the proceeds of the sale of the house, she plans to buy a flat big enough for the three of them after paying off the debts. Make fresh FDs. He had even prematurely enchased their insurance policies; she has to now invest in health and life insurance again.

Life had dealt her a huge blow. But like a phoenix, she needed to rise from the ashes and rebuild their lives. A strength that she didn't know she possessed propelled her forward. She had to walk a path that she had never envisioned for herself.

The priority now was to get children out of this trauma, this awful shock they had received. They were still bewildered by the change in the family set-up; their father leaving the house, their mother's face devoid of cheer and happiness, the change in their circumstances, the house crawling with people carrying official-looking papers and documents... it was too much for their young minds to grasp. She had to normalize things as fast as she could.

Gathering herself together, she drew in a big breath and readied herself for the rocky journey ahead.

Meet the Co-Authors

Maj Gen (Dr) Beji Mathews, Indian Army (Retd)

Having retired from Army after almost four decades of service across various regions of the country, Beji has settled to a life of quiet—thinking & penning down his thoughts. With a MSc degree, a Post Graduate Diploma in Human Resources Development and having acquired a PhD degree in Management from Guru Kashi University, Punjab, he is a keen educator and plans to get into academic management. An enthusiastic and vibrant individual, with a passion for learning, he has spent a major part of his life mentoring individuals of various ages. A free thinker and intellectual he often dabbles in writing. Having written a few papers in management, he plans to write more on human relations and related issues. Outside his professional endeavours, he enjoys playing golf & sailing.

Col Gaurav Bhatia, PhD (Retd)

Col Gaurav Bhatia, PhD (Retired) is a Scholar Warrior with three decades of expertise in Disaster Management (DM) and Disaster Risk Reduction (DRR), specifically CBRN aspects of anthropogenic disasters. He holds a Doctorate and four Post Graduate Degrees, including a Master's in Disaster Management (Gold Medal). He excelled in the Executive Management Programme at IIM Lucknow and published "Biological Disasters—The City Beautiful (Un)Prepared," the recommendations of the book have been incorporated in the Chandigarh Disaster Management Plan. His writings extensively feature in anthologies and peer-reviewed journals. Notably, he is also listed as a consultant for DM/DRR and WaSH by UNICEF.

Col Arun Hariharan (Retd)

Arun Hariharan is an Indian Army veteran & an author, poet and travel blogger based out of New Delhi, India. His best-selling collection of Short Stories titled "A Baker's Dozen—13 Chilling Indian Tales of Macabre" which incorporated three of his passions—travel, history and exploring local legends—as published in 2021. His works-both short stories and poetry, have also been published over 30 times in a number of international anthologies. One of his poems published in the UK was appreciated by King Charles III and Princess Anne, the Princess Royal.

Vivek Gulati

Born in a Forest officer's family meant living in tough conditions. Taught by his mother at home till class 1st as there were no schools nearby, he has seen how she supported his father in bringing up their children with best possible education and values. As an Advertising professional he enjoyed writing ad headlines, ad copy etc.

He started writing on topics close to his heart and the poems that came about have a fair share of his experiences. He has also written for anthologies like "Women vs We Men", "Second Innings", "Coupled Uncoupled" and "Yin and Yang for ILPH and "The Marital

Games" and "Quarantine Days" for Inkfeathers Publishing.

The pandemic gave Vivek enough time to further develop his interest and he has off late contributed quite a bit for Story Mirror writing poems. He writes in English and Hindi. His motto is to concentrate on quality and on topics close to heart.... Dil se!

Dr. Raj Shankar Ghosh

Raj Shankar Ghosh is a public health physician with more than three decades of delivering primary health care across India and South Asian countries. He was born in a small district town, Jalpaiguri in North Bengal. Raj Shankar studied in boarding schools that were run by Jesuit priests in his childhood and in later years in a Rama Krishna Mission run boarding school in Kolkata. In his growing up years, Raj Shankar was exposed to a multicultural environment that taught him tolerance and the value of inclusiveness in life.

In his work life, Raj Shankar has lived in multiple tiers of cities and district towns across States in India. In these villages, small towns and large Metros of India, Raj Shankar has discovered the plots and characters of his stories. These stories have shaped up his thinking and his trust in the incredible India that he believes he is fortunate to be a citizen of.

Raj Shankar has published a book of anecdotes from his public health journey. The book is accessible free of cost at https://lovingvaccines.co.in.

Ramya V

Ramya V is an IT professional who delves into the world of books. A voracious reader who believes the pen is mightier to bring about a change. She has contributed and won as a co-author to more than forty anthologies in prose and poetry. She received a certification of appreciation for her poem in the Annual Wordsmith Award 2021 hosted by Asian Literary Society. She is also the editor of two poetry anthologies and one story anthology. She was shortlisted for the Orange Flower Awards 2022 hosted by Women's Web. In 2022 and 2023 she received certificate of excellence awarded for "Indian Women Rising Star" under the category 'Literature' from Asian Literary Society. In 2023 she received the "Sarojini Naidu—Iconic Women Achiever" award.

Monika Patel

A Learning Specialist by profession, Monika works with Children with Special Needs (CWSN) and their parents. Her decision to work in the field of remedial education and take a degree to aid the same has been a journey down an untrodden path no less.

Monika took to writing for anthologies during the pandemic. Her short stories and poems have been published in anthology collections of publications like—Impish Lass Publishing House and Inkfeathers Publishing. Along with her private practice currently she is a consultant at an NGO. Apart from writing she engages in reading and sketching in her leisure time.

Zeyd Ladha

Zeyd Ladha is a writer and entrepreneur hailing from the vibrant city of Mumbai. With his effortless writing style, he seamlessly blends simplicity and sophistication, leaving an indelible mark on the reader's mind. His work has been featured in various anthologies and magazines, showcasing his versatility in writing articles, stories, and poems. Through his writing, Zeyd aims to inspire and motivate his readers, often weaving in profound messages of hope and positivity. He draws inspiration from the nuances of everyday life, using his keen observation skills to impart knowledge and wisdom to his readers. He recently launched his debut poetry book. Odyssey—of life, of learnings, of joy, which won the certificate of excellence in the best debut poetry book category at Asian Literary Society's prestigious meet.

Rita Som

Rita Som hails from Ambernath a small industrial township near Mumbai, now settled in Pallava, Dombivili. She is a Graduate in Psychology and Post Graduate in English literature and did her B.Ed. from Mumbai University. She started her career as a lecturer in a college teaching English Language and retired as the principal of a school. She is a prolific writer and many of her stories and articles are published. She is one of the esteemed writers for The Impish Lass Publishing House and is in the team of editors 23-24 working on the Young Bard Project.

Mehak Lakhwani

Mehak Lakhwani has been writing since her early days and has co-authored more than 15 anthologies for The Impish Lass and Inkfeathers. She loves composing poems and stories that are mostly poignant in nature and penning flawed jarring communal eventualities in their rawest form which are often a reflection of her foregoing experiences. This expression to emote is truly cathartic to her. Reading Greek and Roman mythologies and watching psychological thrillers is her favourite recipe to rejuvenate and acquire ingenuity in mapping out her upcoming oeuvres. Her father always believed in her power of pen and kept encouraging, but she took up writing only recently after his demise. She thanks him every day for lighting up her path in this direction.

Vasudha Kapoor Duggal

An alumna of Loreto Convent Kolkata, Vasudha graduated in Political Science from Kolkata University and did her Management from IGNOU. She has a rich corporate experience of more than 25 years across 4 leading private companies and an MNC. She took an early retirement from her corporate career to pursue other interests and also work in the social sector. She is a Trustee in a renowned NGO and actively involved in its various programmes on education, culture and heritage. She has about six poetry & story anthologies to her credit and an e-zine where her poem was published. Vasudha now lives in Gurgaon with her family and can be reached at vasudha1608@gmail.com.

Aditi Lahiry

Aditi Lahiry is an English and French Language Teacher. She is passionate about writing poems, stories and articles. Many of her works has been published in various anthologies like Airavata and Pegasus by Mayaakatha and Pachyderm tales, published by Ukiyoto Publishers, My Covid Diary published by Inkfeathers Publishers. She lives in Hyderabad with her family.

Binta Elsa Biju

Binta Elsa Biju is a post graduate in English Language and Literature, who is an ardent admirer of art and literature. She is a passionate soul, eagerly wishing to be an advocate of fruitful thoughts and actions. She is fond of reading, writing poems and exploring novel areas of literature that grab her attention.

Shirley Verghese

It has been seven years since her retirement and Shirley has been able to pick up various interests. At 67, Shirley is enjoying a content life after a long career of 38 years with the Reserve Bank of India. She now dabbles in writing, reading, travelling, listening to music, and cooking. Always in the student mode, curious to learn, she picks up courses into the study of

Ancient History, Mythology and Philosophy.

She loves to write mostly for herself, poems and stories that reflect some of her personal life experiences in her journey. She has contributed for more than twenty odd anthologies published by the Impish Lass Publications.

She is a qualified Psychotherapist, passionate about counselling those who approach her, listening and helping them find their path to meaningful living.

Asad Chaugule

Asad is an Automotive Surface designer by profession, along with an interest in sketching cars, Asad has a flair for writing poems in English and Urdu and goes by the penname of Assad Omar. Asad loves exploring nature to enhance his creative skills in designing and writing.

Kirti V

IT professional turned teacher, Ms Kirti took to writing during the pandemic of 2020. She continues to learn the nuances of poetry, prose, and story writing. Her poems have been published in anthologies across languages. She is the recipient of the Literoma Author of the Year 2021 award, NE8X Tagore Commemorative 2022 and Author Awardee and Sahityakosh Samman, NE8X LitFest Author of the Year 2023, The Little Booktique Hub Best Rhymer 2022, Ukiyoto Poet of the Year 2022, Orange Flower Awards nominee of 2021, 2022 and 2023. Her debut poetry book Tides of Life was published in January 2022 and has won the certificate of excellence from Asian Literary Society. Her works can be read at www.kirtisignature.com.

Anthony Fernandes

Anthony Savio Herminio da Piedade Fernandes is a Researcher, Poet and Educationist. He is the Founder Owner of Trading Equations and works at Philu's Farm. He has attended and participated in over 300 workshops. He is a domain scholar in Economics and Finance, Marketing and Patent & IPR. He has completed over 100 certificate courses apart from 4 Post-graduate Degrees. He has over 35 chapters published in national and international ISBN books with a research paper. His subjects of study are usually Social Science topics. He is a Roman Catholic by religion and respects other religions as well. He loves pets and gardening. He supports green environment and chemical-free organic farming.

Dr. Neelam Singh

Dr Neelam Singh is a medical graduate—MBBS from Grant Medical College & JJ group of Hospitals, Mumbai India. She has practiced for about 40 years without a break. She always had a literary bent and is interested in writing poems and article. As an active member of Inner wheel Club of Ambernath, India & as the past president has contributed her writings for this forum. As a member of Indian Medical Association, she has put in her articles in there also.

Neelam now divides her time between her visits to USA and U.K to be with her daughters and grandchildren. Also travelling around the world at large she would like to devote more time to her creative side.

Smriti Agarwal

An active leader, associate editor, author, columnist for newspaper, parent and teacher mentor, Smriti Agarwal is a multiple award-winning early childhood educator since the year 1995,

Writing is a love for her which won her an award from Scholastic India for writing on the topic 'The School of my Dreams'. Her published work includes numerous articles in educational journals/magazines, articles and stories in anthologies. She is the academic council member of GFECER, West Zonal Head for ECDF (Early Child Development Forum), Assistant General Manager Pre-primary Curriculum and a teacher mentor with Madhuban Educational Books.

Ishita Sharma

Ishita Sharma belongs to the 'City of Forts', Jaipur. She expresses herself freely since her childhood but started penning her thoughts when she became fifteen. She is a feminist, fiction writer and a person who expresses her inner volcano through writing. For her listening music is most effective for a person to be calm and nothing can cheer her more than a cold coffee and chocolates. Her love is to express her thoughts without any hesitation.

Dr. Neeta Ranbhan

Dr Neeta Ranbhan is a dental surgeon by profession having her own private practice since last 34 years in Ambernath. Dr Neeta is happily married to her Dr Kamlesh Ranbhan who is into Research and development and a PhD in pharmaceutical chemistry.

She has been the founder editor and past president of Indian Dental Association. She is also a founder member and editor of Ambernath Medical Association and past president of Inner Wheel Club of Ambernath and a volunteer of Art of Ving foundation and an ardent follower of the Sri Sri Ravi Shankar ji, founder of AOL

She is blessed with a daughter Rumjhum, also a practising Dental surgeon. Dr Neeta's hobbies include reading, travelling, painting and socialising and tries to follow a yoga way of life with meditation, pranayaams and yogasanas as part of her daily practice.

Rupali Samant

Rupali Samant is happily married and a mother of two children. She believes and always tells herself that "Strength comes from within. Do not look outside of you." She's a professional certified Fitness coach, a Personal Counsellor and Mindful Meditation coach. She trains in strength training, weight training, pilates, power yoga, core cardio workouts, kettlebell training, kickboxing, and with dancing training as well. She's currently doing so through virtual online sessions. She is an Ultra marathoner who loves to run.

Praneel Dev

"Words are our more inexhaustible source of magic."—Albus Dumbledore. The author is a firm believer in the strength and magnificence of books, writing and literature. He prefers to spend his time delving into new worlds and losing himself in fantasy.

Augusta Vimla Vincent

Augusta Vimla Vincent is a retired English teacher. From childhood, she has had a craving for language and literature. Post retirement, she has taken up writing as her hobby. She loves writing poems and has written for six anthologies till now and two e-books. She writes for both Impish lass Publishing House and Inkfeathers Publishing.

Rhythmi Rosa S.

Rhythmi Rosa S is a writer from India. She has completed her B.Com and currently works at an MNC. She loves writing poetry, articles, quotes and short stories. She has won first place in poetry competitions twice during her college days. Currently she writes for poetry anthologies.

www.ingramcontent.com/pod-product-compliance
Lightning Source LLC
LaVergne TN
LVHW010555160826
845677LV00013B/3141